HIGHLAND
DREAMER

WILLA BLAIR

OLIVERHEBERBOOKS

To friends, old and new.

ACKNOWLEDGMENTS

To everyone at Oliver-Heber Books, to all of my readers, my critique partners, and my Beta readers, a big thank you from me! My readers encourage me to write, my critique partners keep me on track, my Beta readers keep my plot on track, my editors keep me from making mistakes of every kind, and my publisher keeps my books coming out to my readers who encourage me to write the next book...and so it goes. It's a perfect circle of creativity!

PROLOGUE

SCOTTISH HIGHLANDS, LATE SUMMER 1539

Tavish Lathan moved within the Aerie's walls so smoothly, he seemed to float, much as he had every other time he found himself in this strangely altered place. He drifted at the will of something he did not control. The wind? Nay. Banners hung from tower tops unruffled by any breeze. He approached the gate, then went back the other way, deeper into the bailey. He couldn't see anyone. No people. No animals. Not even a butterfly or a bird. He was utterly alone. Where was the lass?

Then he saw her. Tall and lithe, she stepped away from him, her russet dress rippling with her movement. Her long brown hair hung down her back in a thick braid shot through with highlights the color of bronze metal, swaying with each step. Left. Right. His gliding progress fell into the pattern of the swing of her hair and his view narrowed to her. Only her.

He followed, edging ever nearer. Perhaps this time, he would come close enough to touch her. To make her stop, face him, and tell him why she appeared in his visions again and again, at first from a distance, but by now, almost in reach.

She glanced over her shoulder. The corner of her mouth visible in *profile lifted as if she knew he was following her and could hear his thoughts.*

Heat flared deep in his chest as he imagined her smile. Desire grew stronger each time he dreamed and came closer to her. If only she would turn and face him, he might discover who she was. Even the slight glimpse she gave him made his blood sizzle. He envisioned her as more beguiling than any lass he'd ever seen, with milky skin and warm brown eyes, lips the perfect rosy shade of a Highland sky at sunrise, pink, lush and lovely.

She paused, and with the same teasing glance, lifted one hand. Her fingers curled, and then fell gently to her side.

Was she beckoning him, or did she mean to warn him away? Tavish wanted to growl in frustration, but he couldn't make a sound. Instead, he drifted after her, unable to close the last, tormenting distance between them. Until, with a final enigmatic glance over her shoulder, she turned a corner and disappeared. As soon as he lost sight of her, his dreamlike progress stopped.

Icy tendrils of fear replaced the burning desire that drove him to pursue her. Why couldn't he reach her? What purpose did she serve in his vision? And would he ever meet her in the real world?

1

Tavish surged up in bed, gasping for air, every muscle tensed with effort. It had happened again. As it had a dozen times before, the lass he wanted to see again, preferably in the here and now, had appeared. Only this time, she beckoned him to follow her—but where? Or had she urged him to stay back?

He rubbed his eyes, trying to drive away the last vestiges of the unsettling night. The questions her presence raised left him with a sense of foreboding that twisted his belly and drove him to his feet, tossing aside his blankets. Was she trying to warn of some danger?

He scrubbed his hands over his face. Without success, he'd been searching for the meaning of these visions for weeks. He believed he'd seen her too many times for her appearances to be simple fantasy. What was his Seer's talent trying to show him? The sense of foreboding that overwhelmed him each time he entered the strange dream warred with the desire he felt for her form, her grace, the luster of her dark brown hair, and for answers to the mystery she represented. What about her kept his dreams disquieting and his belly in knots?

With a groan, he noted the glow leaking in around the shutter covering his window. Morning had come. It was still early, but he had no interest in sleeping any longer. He pulled on his clothes, vowing to find a way to take control, to summon her to face him the next time he slept, and to speak to him. If he could dominate the dream-world, he could get the answers he wanted.

He might soon get the help he needed. His mother had requested that the MacKyrie Seer and Laird, Ellie MacKyrie, meet with him to help him master his talent, or at least to understand and interpret what he had seen again and again these last few weeks. If the apprehension each vision left him with was tied to something yet to occur, any help she could give him couldn't happen soon enough.

As he tucked his dirk into his belt, the thought of the MacKyrie Seer coming for the lairds' gathering made him wonder if he'd seen the lass because she, too, would soon arrive for the same event. If so, no matter who she came with, or why she was here, Tavish would find her.

Resolved, he headed downstairs.

"There ye are," his twin sister Eilidh remarked as he entered the herbal. "Ye are early. Did ye have another dream?" She slid off her stool and approached him, her gaze locked with his, concern furrowing her brow.

"Aye." He didn't want to talk about it, but Eilidh would not accept his silence where his burgeoning talent and mysterious visions were concerned. Before he could distract her by asking what tasks they'd been set this morning, she continued to probe.

"With the same beautiful lass?"

Tavish grimaced. Eilidh was forever trying to find him a lass to love. She thought him too solitary, too lonely. How anyone could think that in this family, in this tightly-knit clan, was more than he could comprehend. "I still havena seen her face, only a glimpse of part of her profile."

"Still, perhaps ye have finally seen yer one true love," she said and put a hand on his arm.

He glanced at it, then lifted and dropped it. "And perhaps ye are as daft as—well, I canna think of anything quite as daft as ye."

"And if I'm daft, what does that make ye, brother?"

"Yer keeper?" Her snort told him he'd convinced her she'd dispelled the gloom that often hung over him after one of these visions.

"Not a chance," she challenged and tossed a rag at him, then gestured to the table beside her. "I've begun the next batch of tisane Mother requested. Why not make yourself useful and find the comfrey for it. I've looked, but either Mother used it all, or distracted, she's tucked it away and forgotten to tell us where she put it."

Tavish opened the cabinet where their mother stored fresh herbs as well as finished potions. "Ye mean *this* comfrey?" He reached in and plucked a bunch, tied with string, that had gotten pushed to the back of the top shelf.

"Aye. Where was it?"

"Where ye are tall enough ye shouldha seen it. Perhaps mother is not the only one distracted lately."

He handed her the bundle of herbs and perched on a nearby stool. "Still got yer eye on that secret someone whose name ye willna share with me?" If she continued to insist on making the dream lass his future lover, he could return the favor.

"There is no secret someone." She canted her head at the cabinet. "Perhaps ye have a touch of Drummond's talent for finding things." She sniffed, turned her back and began stripping leaves from the stems.

"Ye canna convince me ye are not interested in someone,

my dearest twin." Tavish leaned his elbows on the table. "In all our twenty years together—or a wee bit longer if ye count our time in the womb—I've never seen ye lost in thought like ye have been lately. Ye startle when someone comes to the door, as if ye are hoping for a certain someone."

"I'm yer only twin," she chided. "And ye do the same," she declared, still refusing to look at him.

"Ah, but I do it for a very different reason. I'm trained to be alert and ready to fight. Ye dinna have that excuse. So, tell me, Eilidh. Who is he?"

"Ye are the only distraction plaguing me this morning. If ye canna tell me more about the vision ye had, either start working or leave. Mother will be down soon, and ye ken she wants the herbal well stocked with finished potions before our visitors arrive."

In a few days, their father and eldest brother would be engaged with the gathering of lairds who had signed their father's treaty. After the battle at Flodden Field in 1513 cost Scotland its King, many of its nobles, and most of the lairds and fighting men from its clans, Toran, the new Laird Lathan, had conceived a treaty to unite the local clans in a pact of mutual defense. He had intended to see that clan rivalries and feuds died with the old lairds and their heirs. At his encouragement, the younger sons and daughters who, like him, had never expected to inherit their new responsibilities, banded together against incursions from the Lowlands, the English, and even other Highland clans. For more than twenty years, the treaty had worked.

But unrest among the Highland clans prompted him to call the gathering to renew the bonds that had kept them all safe and prosperous since those dark days. The news from King James V's court that he intended to subdue the western Highland and Island lairds made the local clans worry that they would be next. Some even insisted that the treaty made them more likely to come under royal scrutiny and suggested dissolving it. Toran still believed they were stronger together, even if they bent the knee to the King. Trouble had come from many directions in the years since Flodden. No one was foolish enough to think that would end any time soon.

Tavish fully supported what his father had done, and the purpose of the gathering, but he expected to have a minor role at most. His eldest brother, Drummond, was the heir and would sit at their father's side during the lairds' discussions.

The mention of their arriving visitors turned Tavish's thoughts back to the lass in his vision. "I wonder who she is," he said as he went to do as Eilidh bid.

"If she is coming to the gathering, ye will find out soon enough," Eilidh said to his back, then she added, "I canna wait to meet my new sister."

The smirk in her tone was unmistakable. "Eilidh," Tavish said, twisting to face her, his tone full of menace to make her leave off teasing him. "Not another word, and certainly not to anyone else. Ye ken how fast tales travel in this clan."

She sighed and gave him an apologetic look. "I do. Yer secret is safe with me as long as ye wish it to be."

YVAINE MACKYRIE LEFT HER CHAMBER ON HER WAY DOWN TO THE MacKyrie great hall to break her fast. She'd been drawn by the mouth-watering scents of roasted meat and fresh bread wafting up the stairs. But she paused in the hallway when her father, Donal MacNabb, stepped out of the chamber he shared with her mother, Ellie, the MacKyrie Laird and Seer. He held up a finger to silence Yvaine until he gently tugged the door closed.

"How is she?" Yvaine's belly dropped when her father's gaze shifted from hers to the floor.

"She's in some pain again today. I told her to rest a wee

longer. 'Tis a good thing, I think, that we're leaving tomorrow for the Aerie. Aileana will see to her and put a stop to this."

"'Tis only been a few weeks—"

"Nay, daughter." He took her arm and turned her toward the stairs. Escorting her? Or needing the reassurance of her touch? "She's had the belly pain for months, but hid it until it became strong enough she could nay longer keep it her own secret. Why she didna send for Aileana Lathan much sooner..." He paused and shook his head as they started down the steps. "Yer mother is as stubborn a lass as I've ever kenned."

"Likely she learned some of that from ye, Da."

"And ye and yer brother inherited a full measure from both of us."

Yvaine appreciated that he summoned a smile to soften any sting his words might have caused. But the news about her mother hollowed her belly.

They reached the great hall in time for serving lasses to bring out platters of bread, butter, cheese, sliced venison, honey and dark, purple berries from the nearby brambles. Yvaine's appetite had fled with her father's admission that her mother had been ill for much longer than she knew. From his frown and hooded gaze as he surveyed what was offered, he'd lost his appetite as well.

"Walk with me," she suggested, putting a hand on his arm. "We're neither of us ready for this meal."

He nodded and turned with her toward the keep's heavy oaken door. The air was crisp in the inner bailey. Snow had not yet begun to drape the surrounding peaks in sparkling white, but winter was not far off in this part of the Highlands. Not long after it made its presence known, the passes into their glen would become difficult to negotiate, or even impassable. If Mother was truly very ill, taking her to the Aerie needed to happen soon, and not just for the Lathan laird's gathering.

Yvaine hated to add to her father's somber mood, but she

had to tell him what she'd seen. What she feared. As he led her toward the stables, she began. "Ye ken I want to go to the Aerie with ye."

"Ye do?"

"Dinna think to tease me out of this. Ye havena forgotten. I ken ye too well for ye to be able to deceive me. But I havena told ye why. Da, I've had a vision."

He turned and snapped his gaze to her. "Yer mother?"

"Nay, it concerns ye. Ye will be in danger there."

"Nonsense. I spent years at Lathan. I'm as much family there as here."

"But there will be more than Lathans at the gathering. There will be strangers from other clans, and not just the lairds. Their guards. Likely, others, too. And I havena seen where the danger comes from. I must go with ye, to be able to warn ye, when I do."

"Yer mother can do that."

"Nay, she hasna seen what I have seen. I think the valerian tisane she drinks to help her sleep keeps her visions from her. She's had nay warnings."

"Or perhaps, there is nay danger. Ye have said what ye see in yer dreams does not always come to be. Or that ye dinna always ken how to interpret them."

"Aye, that is true. But..." She paused and clenched her fist in front of her belly. "The feeling I have here has not gone away. My visions have been too vague to be helpful. I've seen only symbols of danger. A blade, glimpses of indistinct weapons, and solitary predators under a full moon." She shrugged. "My belly is filled with buzzing bees, yet all I can do is wait for the reason to become clear."

"Ye are anxious about being left here in the charge of yer brother. Because ye fear if ye dream true, he might soon become yer laird, and his first act will be to marry ye off so ye canna continue to torment him."

"Da! Dinna even think that ye both willna return." She paused and put a restraining hand on his arm and met his gaze when he stopped and turned to her. "But think on this—if ye leave me here, if I canna reach ye in time..." She let go of his arm, wrapped her arms around herself and studied the ground, then looked up at him. "Ye mean more to me than anyone in the world. I willna lose ye if I can do anything to save ye."

"I mean more to ye than yer mother?"

His eyes held a twinkle that hadn't been there a few moments before.

"Da! Be serious. Take me with ye. If for no other reason than Mother may need my help." If he wouldn't believe her for his own sake, he might agree for her mother's.

"She has me for that."

"And if she has to spend time with the healer, ye will be busy at the gathering in her stead. I can help—both of ye."

They walked on in silence for a dozen paces, then her father dropped a heavy arm around her shoulders, pulled her against his side and sighed. "Very well. Ye may come. But ye will be careful. Those same strangers who concern ye will be more likely to be interested in a beautiful lass than in an old warrior."

"Ye are not old."

"Older than ye, lass."

"I should hope so! Ye are my da. Or is there something ye and mother havena told me."

He chuckled at that. "Nay, Yvaine. Ye are my one true daughter. I love ye. And yer brother. As much as I love yer mother." He lifted her chin with a curled finger. "I willna stand by and lose ye, either, lass. If I deem it needful, I will assign a guard to ye."

She hated the idea of being escorted everywhere she wanted to go. Any sense of confinement chilled her. "If ye are family to the Lathans, that means I am, too. If ye are perfectly safe, I will be."

"If I deem it needful, ye willna argue with my decision, or I'll lock ye in a chamber until 'tis time to return home."

Yvaine hid a shudder. She knew he meant every word and would do exactly what he threatened.

———

THREE LONG DAYS LATER, AS SHE LIFTED WIND-BLOWN HAIR OUT of her eyes, Yvaine realized her father's descriptions, while generally accurate, did nothing to evoke the majesty of the Aerie. It sat atop a high, steep-sided tor, and reached even higher into the gloaming, a ghostly full moon floating just beyond and above its towers, lights glinting through diamond-paned windows at the top. Torches lined the crenellated defensive walls. She'd never believed a place could look so magical. The Aerie was much as her father had told her, and yet—much more.

He'd said the MacKyrie keep was larger, and perhaps it was, or simply more spread out in its glen, its dimensions unconstrained by the sides of a steep hill. They reached a fast-flowing burn and crossed it without incident into a wide glen bordered by forests. More mountains loomed beyond them. There, above her, she saw the path to the Aerie's gates, rising long and narrow along a cliff. Surely no more than two horses could ride abreast. Perhaps not even that many. She shivered at the thought of riding that trail herself. Now she could see why the siege she'd been told about had failed. The Aerie was unassailable—from without.

But with strangers inside its walls? Perhaps not. Was that the source of her foreboding? Not a danger directed specifically at her father, but at the Lathans, and at the Aerie, too? That thought gave her no comfort. Her father would defend his friends, she had no doubt. Even to the death.

She was here to see that didn't happen.

A few tents were already set up in the glen. The MacKyrie party was not the first to arrive. Who was here? And whom would she meet during the next few days? She'd rarely ventured outside the MacKyrie glen, except to help with whisky deliveries when her father judged the trip safe enough for a lass to go along. Usually then, he doubled the guard. She'd never traveled so far from home. Being this far from MacKyrie was exciting—and terrifying, too, but she reveled in the sense of freedom it gave her.

At her father's direction, their guards split off into the glen to set up their camp. Donal pointed out the best ground for a defensive perimeter and, in case they had to respond to trouble, quick access to the trail up the tor. They would remain in the glen unless on duty serving her parents, or if trouble arose.

At the base of the trail, she pulled up, hesitant to attempt the climb. But a glance aside at her parents sitting confidently on their favorite mounts calmed her. Her mother met her gaze with a smile, then nodded to her father. Yvaine was certain he would choose to stay alongside her mother, but without a word, she'd directed him to care for his daughter. He guided his mount along Yvaine's, one of the guards took up position by her mother, and they proceeded.

She kept her gaze on the gates above her as they rode up the narrow path. She dared not look aside, or worse, down, or she'd lose her seat on her horse. And as frightening as riding up the tor must be, leaving the Aerie would be worse. She'd have nowhere to look but down. If she lost her balance, she'd fall. No one would survive such a fall. She closed her eyes on a shudder, then lifted her gaze.

The pale moon hovered just over the shoulder of the keep. The sensation of changing tides was strong and Yvaine shivered. It wasn't a vision, exactly, but a sensation this strong was something akin to one, and something her mother often described as the forewarning of a vision that might provide the answers she needed. As they, at last, passed under the portcullis and through the open gates, Yvaine hoped her mother was right.

She glanced aside to ensure that her mother had made the trip up the tor unscathed.

Ellie's gaze was fixed on the steps leading into the main keep. A woman stood there, tall, beautiful and serene. The Lathan lady? When her father waved, he confirmed her suspicion. This was the Lathan healer, Aileana Shaw.

Yvaine dismounted and handed her mount's reins off to a lad who'd run out from the stable.

Donal dismounted and went to his wife to help her down. He nodded to the lad and gave him the reins of his horse and her mother's, as well. He took Ellie's arm and led her to the steps. Yvaine followed close behind.

Aileana came down the steps and greeted them. "Donal. 'Tis years since last we saw ye here. Ye look well."

"Well enough, Healer. Ye have never met my wife, Ellie."

"I'm pleased to finally meet ye. After years of letters shared between us, 'tis good to see ye."

"And I, ye. Donal didna do ye justice."

Aileana laughed, a musical sound that pleased Yvaine's ears.

"I am not surprised. Donal and I have long traded barbs."

"And my daughter, Yvaine," her father interrupted, ignoring the healer's statement and making Yvaine want to hear more.

"I'm pleased to meet ye, Lady Lathan." The healer's reputation was well-known at MacKyrie. Yvaine was tempted to bow, but held herself upright.

Aileana smiled at her. "Ye could be the daughter of no others than these two," she said and gestured at Yvaine's parents. "Beautiful like yer mother, and, I suspect, proud like yer sire. Do ye carry the same gift?"

"She does," Ellie said, softly. "Though imperfectly as yet. It grows stronger."

"And ye do not," Aileana said, and reached out a hand, but did not quite touch Ellie. "Ye are in pain. Come, we must get ye settled. Ye have missed the evening meal, but I'll have Cook prepare some food and drink for ye. We can speak later."

Donal cleared his throat, a gruff sound against the soft assurance of the healer's voice, and nodded.

Aileana conducted them into the keep, through the great hall where she asked a lass to pass her instructions to Cook, and up a set of stairs to a hallway that led to a large chamber with plush chairs before the hearth and a table and chairs near the window. Beyond that, a connecting chamber contained a grand bed, chest, and cheery fire glowing in the hearth. "I hope ye will be comfortable here. Yvaine, ye will take the smaller chamber across the hall. She will be close by," Aileana added when Donal's head came up. "*Dinna fash.*"

He nodded. "Well enough. Yvaine, go see to yer chamber."

He said it kindly, but she recognized a dismissal when she heard it. Whatever he wished to say, he didn't want her to hear. She nodded and went across the hall, but left the door open, knowing sounds would carry in these stone walls as they did at MacKyrie. She and her brother Michiel had often used that to their advantage, overhearing much they were not meant to know.

"Aileana, ye must..."

"I ken it, Donal. I can see Ellie isna well. Ye will leave her to my care and go on about MacKyrie business for her. Toran is eager to see ye. He'll be in his solar at this hour."

"I am nay as sick as all that," Yvaine heard her mother say.

"Let Aileana care for ye," Donal said so softly, Yvaine almost missed the pleading in his voice. "Love, she will help ye."

Yvaine heard the door across the hall close and his heavy tread approaching. Her mother must have given her agreement. She hurried further into her chamber, nearly tripping over a small table as she pivoted around the chair next to it.

Donal entered and looked around, then met her gaze. "Does this suit ye?"

She nodded at the window that kept the chamber from feeling closed in. Moonlight painted a bright stripe across the single bed opposite the cheery hearth. "It does, Da. Will the healer be able to help mother?"

"If anyone can, Aileana can. *Dinna fash*."

"Then ye must cease as well."

He gave her a thin smile. "Stay close by in case yer mother or the healer call for ye," he said, then left her to settle into her new surroundings.

2

Y vaine paced from the window to the door and back again, a grand journey of eight steps in each direction and a pivot on the ball of her foot. She'd spent the last hour waiting patiently in the small chamber she'd been given, putting away the few belongings she'd brought after the servants carried them up to her, but she'd had enough. Any kind of confinement set her teeth on edge. Perhaps it was time to see what was keeping her mother and the Lathan healer. She hadn't heard a sound. The woman could not have left the chamber across the hall without her knowing.

She opened her door and peered out. The hallway was empty and her parents' chamber door was still closed. She slipped out of her room and pulled the door softly shut behind her, then crossed the hall and leaned an ear against her parents' door. She didn't hear anything, so she opened it, just a crack, thinking perhaps they had gotten by her. When no one called out, she opened the door fully and stepped in. Seeing no one, she went to the inner door.

Her mother lay on the bed in the inner chamber, and appeared to be asleep. The healer sat in a chair by the bed, close enough to hold her mother's hand. She looked up as Yvaine entered, and beckoned her in. "She's resting," the healer told her softly, almost in a whisper. "I'm glad ye are here. I must go, but I didna wish to leave her alone."

"Is she well?"

The healer's hand dropped to her own abdomen, then quickly lifted away before she answered. "She is better, but there is more I must do another day."

"Tomorrow?"

"Aye, most likely." She placed Ellie's hand on the bed and stood.

Yvaine moved around her and took the seat she vacated. "I'll stay with her. What will she need when she awakens?"

"Food and drink. I hope her appetite will be restored, at least in some small measure."

"I, too. She's gotten too thin."

"Well, we'll see what we can do about that. By now, Cook will have prepared something for all of ye."

Hunger was the last thing Yvaine cared about at the moment. "Do ye ken what has pained her?"

"Aye. In some, the monthly flux escapes into the belly where it attaches to a lass's insides and continues to bleed with her moon cycles, or it sticks together parts that should not be joined. That is the source of her pain. I have begun to remove the flux tissue from where it doesna belong, but 'tis a slow process. Dinna fash, lass. She will be well." Her smile came and went so quickly, Yvaine might have imagined it. "I'll check on her later," she added.

Yvaine realized she looked tired, even in pain, her hand over her belly much as her mother had often done these last weeks—even months. She had been told the healer took each illness or injury from her patient into herself, but she hadn't believed it—until now. Words seemed inadequate, but they were all she had. "Thank ye, Healer."

Aileana nodded and left.

Yvaine studied her mother. Asleep, she seemed more at ease than she had in a long time. Ellie MacKyrie was the strongest woman Yvaine knew, yet only now did she realize how she'd weakened over time, with tiredness and pain taking their toll on her. If the Lathan healer could help her, Yvaine would be eternally grateful. She could not bear the thought of losing her mother. Not only for herself, but for her father.

She couldn't begin to imagine how he would react. To her father, the sun rose and set with her mother and always had, since the day he first saw her, though he claimed to recall it differently. Yvaine had heard the story of their courtship. Her mother had seen Donal MacNabb in her dreams, though not clearly. Then one day, he and several other men showed up. They had saved a wagon-load of MacKyrie whisky—and the old men and lads taking it to market—from bandits. At first, she hadn't been sure which of the Lathan visitors had been the one reaching for her in her dreams, but it didn't take long to become clear. It took longer for her to win him over, but they'd been happy together for more than twenty years.

Yvaine hoped someday to find a love like that. Someday, but not soon.

She leaned her head against the back of the chair and gave in to the restful quiet.

SHE WAS INSIDE A SPACE BORDERED BY STONE WALLS AND DARKNESS. A hallway? She glanced around. Behind her, a torch glimmered, painting a floor polished by countless steps with an eerie glow. Something glinted, and she turned toward it in time for a shadow to cross the pool of light. Little tingles spread from her belly into her chest. She clenched her fists. Someone was watching her. Following her. She couldn't see who, but she knew someone was there.

Yvaine jerked awake at the sound of the chamber door opening.

Her father stepped in, glanced at her, then settled his gaze on her mother. "Aileana said she made some progress." His shoulders dropped. "Has yer mother been resting this whole time? She looks better, even in sleep."

"I think so. I dozed off after the healer left, until ye arrived. I dinna think she's stirred." She didn't tell him about her dream. Her vision. She didn't know which it was, except that the eerie mood of it made her believe it was the latter. But it told her little. Rather, it made her heart stutter each time she thought about being watched by some hidden stranger. If not for the danger she'd sensed while at home, after that dream, she would wish she'd never come to the Aerie. Her father might feel as though he belonged here, but so far, she did not.

"Lass, Cook has food for us downstairs. I'd take ye down myself and introduce ye to the twins, but I dinna wish to leave yer mother alone. They're about yer age and the lass, Eilidh, could be a friend to ye while we remain."

"Ye dinna need to escort me, Da. I'll be fine." As long as she didn't start jumping at shadows in the corridors.

He smiled and leaned down to kiss her cheek. "Go eat, and maybe ye'll meet Eilidh. She'll look much like Jamie did when he fostered with us. Her twin brother will, too, of course, even more so. Then bring up some food for me and yer mother, aye? She should wake soon."

"I will, Da."

Yvaine left her seat to her father and ventured out into the hall, heart pounding at the reminder of her dream of being watched. She paused, closed her eyes briefly and listened, but sensed nothing. No one else was around. That suited her.

If she hadn't been asked to bring food up to her parents, she'd go back to her chamber. She didn't feel like talking to anybody, or dealing with anyone watching her. But she'd promised. And as soon as the scent of roasting meat greeted her, her belly reminded her it had been hours since she'd broken her fast on the trail. She made her way down the stairs to the great hall.

THE NEXT MORNING, TAVISH AND HIS TWIN SISTER EILIDH WAITED near the Aerie's massive gates as more visitors rode the long trail up the tor. A few had arrived last evening. The majority were due in today.

Much remained to do as lairds began arriving. The rest of the clan was busy preparing sleeping chambers for the lairds, out hunting to supply the larder, or working with Cook to ensure food was ready for any early arrivals. Tavish and Eilidh had been relegated to serve as Lathan greeters, smiles and obsequious attitudes firmly in place. Such ingratiating behavior suited neither him nor his sister.

If Da hadn't ordered the two of them to help the steward by meeting new arrivals, by this time of the morning, Eilidh would be in the herbal working with their mother. Tavish would usually be training with his brother, Drummond, the heir, and oldest of triplets. The exertion of swinging a sword or other weapon helped to tire him and kept dreams at bay. He longed for the exhaustion that let him rest. But until this gathering ended, training would be postponed. Instead, Drummond was with their father, behind closed doors in his solar, meeting with one of the closest of their allies, one of the early arrivals. And Tavish was here.

He frowned. Dreamless sleep was a luxury and training a necessity, except that it might prevent him from learning more about the lass in his visions. But being here did have one distinct advantage. Unless he'd missed the lass before they took up their duty, if she was real and on her way here, he was sure to see her arrive and learn who she was.

"Ach, look who's about to join us," Eilidh said, leaning close and keeping her voice low, her smile fixed in place. "I think that's old laird MacBean. I've heard tales of him."

Tavish's equally vacuous smile turned briefly to a frown before he recovered. "I, too. Keep away from him. He's reputed to like lasses younger than ye, but I willna have ye accosted by him or any other man."

"*Dinna fash*, brother mine. I can take care of myself."

"With a dirk, aye, but he's twice yer weight and more."

"And I'll wager I'm faster."

"Dinna count on it."

"Smile, brother. Here he comes."

Tavish straightened and did as she bade. No matter the provocation, save for assault on his sister, he would not besmirch the Lathan reputation. The MacBean laird had a great deal of influence with some of the clans expected to attend. Tavish did not intend to make his father's job harder by insulting a guest.

With a gesture, Tavish kept Eilidh back and went to greet their newest visitor while two guards dismounted, one on either side of him. "Good day, Laird MacBean."

"'Tis a good day to be off a horse," the laird replied, swinging his bulk to the ground. He handed his reins to the stable lad who ran up to take his horse and those of his men. "Where will I be?"

"Steward is coming," Tavish said amiably, indicated the approaching older man. He kept the relief at the steward's sudden appearance out of his voice by sheer effort. "He will direct ye and yer men. "Pray, how many travel with ye? I must inform the Cook."

"Only these two guards."

"Ye left no men camped in the glen?"

"Nay. My men and I ken how to travel without notice."

Or they were just damned lucky not to have encountered trouble along the way. "Thank ye, sir. Ah, Steward is here." He indicated their latest guests. "Please see to Laird MacBean and his men." He turned back to the visitor. "The steward will take good care of ye, my laird."

Tavish watched them follow the steward into the keep, then returned to where Eilidh waited.

"He never even glanced my way. I must be too old for him."

"Or he's just tired from the journey. Take heed, sister."

"Aye." She punched him in the arm, then stepped to the gate to peer down the tor. "No one else is on the path at the moment. Does Da expect us to stand here all day, waiting?"

"Go rest a wee." He glanced up at the position of the sun. They'd been out here two hours already. "Or see if Mother needs yer help. That is the only excuse I can think of that Da will accept for abandoning this post."

Eilidh would one day replace their mother as the Lathan healer. Though Jamie and Lianna, Drummond's younger triplet siblings, had also inherited a full measure of their mother's healing ability, they both had married outside the clan.

Tavish did what he could to share the burden. Like Drummond, Tavish's healing talents were rudimentary and weak. He spent part of each day in his mother Aileana's herbal, learning from her and trying to strengthen his ability to heal. He enjoyed those sessions. Seeing wounds healed and illnesses cured gave him a sense of accomplishment, but the healer took from the patient the damage and pain of their illness or injury. Thankfully, the harm did not remain with them for long, but while it did, it was exhausting and painful. His mother had done this work for most of her life. His respect for her compassion and strength knew no bounds.

Against the ability to save limbs and lives, his visions seemed much less important. But he knew from his mother's tales about the MacKyrie Seer that visions could reveal much, and save as many or more lives than even a talented healer such as those in his family could do.

Yet, what good was a Seer who could not depend on his visions? Naught that he could see. He was a thinker, a dreamer, a watcher, and only reluctantly a warrior. If only his visions were reliable.

He lived for the day when they would be.

"I'll see what mother is doing, then check on ye before the midday meal, aye?" Eilidh told him. "I willna take long."

Tavish nodded, and she left him to his now solitary duty. He hoped she paid heed to his warnings. By the end of the day, the keep would be full of strange men, and his sister had grown into a beautiful woman.

He noticed Bhaltair enter the keep moments after she did and relaxed. She'd be safe as long as the Lathans' big chief guard stayed nearby.

3

Later, Tavish sat with Bhaltair and two of his men in the great hall watching the serving lasses bring the midday repast from the kitchen. The hall was bustling with the unaccustomed numbers of visitors who'd arrived throughout the morning. All the visiting lairds, save one, were in residence, freeing Tavish from his onerous duty as greeter.

Except to summon him for this meal, Eilidh had never rejoined him. Their mother had kept her busy in the herbal, muttering the entire time about putting their daughter on display for every stranger who rode through their gates. Tavish hoped his father was ready. According to Eilidh, their mother intended to let him know, as soon as they were private, just how daft she thought his order had been. Tavish was fairly certain their father had expected Eilidh to find a way out of it, but didn't want to favor one twin over the other when he gave the order.

Serving lasses moved between tables with alacrity, arms heavily laden with trenchers and hands with cups of ale and cider. According to his father's account, the nine lairds plus their retinues of guards, wives and miscellaneous others added up to more visitors than had ever been inside the Aerie for one occasion.

A lass set a groaning trencher in front of Bhaltair. It looked three times as full as the ones her assistants placed in reach of Tavish and the other guards.

"All we need is a juggler in that corner and a bard with a lute over there," Bhaltair remarked, gesturing with a chicken leg. "Add a tinker and a ribbon-seller wandering about hawking their wares, and we'd have a market day underway here in the hall. We've visitors aplenty. Too many."

Tavish snorted. "Aye, too many. Not that it was a decision left to either of us. Why didna Da insist they limit their party to themselves and a few guards? Well, I do ken why. Mother would never seek to discourage the chance to meet new people. She enjoys it, and considers it part of the education of her twins."

"Twins who are old enough to make bairns of their own," Finn snickered. "I'd think ye two were schooled well enough."

"Ye do ken the Lady Lathan, aye, Finn? Ye've lived here all yer life. There's never an end to learning."

"Aye," Bhaltair said, joining in. "A lesson yer brother Jamie absorbed a bit late. But he learned it." He took a drink. "The MacKyries are here. I wonder if Jamie will visit. That could be an interesting reunion."

"Nay," Tavish said around a mouthful of excellent bread. "The old Keith laird never signed. Nor his heir. They're far enough away, I doubt Jamie would think to bring it up." He shrugged. "Now, Lianna is insatiably curious. Learning was never an issue for her. And look where that got her—wed with David MacDhai. I dinna ken if Drummond will ever approve."

The guard perked up. "Are they coming?"

"Still sweet on her, are ye? She's married, so sod off, aye?" Tavish laughed to soften the criticism, then shrugged. "Nay.

Mother mentioned that MacDhai sent a missive giving Da his proxy. My sister sent her another a few days ago."

Bhaltair's gaze roved the hall while he listened to the conversation. If he ever let his guard down, Tavish had never seen it. And certainly, he wouldn't during this gathering. There were too many strange faces here. Swords of all sizes had been left in the tent camp in the glen, but you could easily kill a man with a dirk—or cut his throat with an eating knife. Bhaltair could do it with his bare hands. Tavish shook his head. When he was younger, the big guard used to scare him, though Bhaltair was only a year or two older than the triplets. But Tavish had known him too long, and seen too many examples of his devotion to their clan—and to Tavish's family—to fear him any longer. Tavish's parents trusted him implicitly. They'd sent him with Lianna when she went with David MacDhai to help save his horses. He'd gone after Drummond when he was late returning from a border village, only to find him delayed by a lass and the search for her missing son.

All Tavish's older siblings were now wed. Neither he nor his twin were in any hurry to join them. At least he wasn't. One could never be sure with a lass. Eilidh might change her mind. But it would take a special lass indeed to change Tavish's.

And there she was!

Tavish sat up straighter. The lass in his dream walked down the stairs. Real. Alive. Coming through the great hall in search of a place to sit, he'd wager. "Look sharp, lads. We're about to have company, and not my sister."

He stood and beckoned the lass. She turned and looked his way. She saw him! He froze, stunned by her beauty and by the intelligence in her warm brown eyes. Then she glanced at his companions and veered toward a table where two Lathan women were eating. Intelligent, indeed.

"Ach, nay," Tavish muttered. "Ye'll not get away from me so easily."

At his elbow, Bhaltair looked up. "What are ye muttering about? Are ye going to sit down and finish yer meal?"

Tavish pushed his trencher toward the big man and stepped over the bench. "Enjoy it. I have something to take care of." He made his way to where the lass sat just as the two women she'd thought to join stood and left her. Tavish grabbed two cups of cider from a passing serving lass and slipped onto the bench across from her. "I'm Tavish," he told her, putting the cups down, one on his side of the table, one on hers. "Ye seemed not to see me invite ye to join us at the other table."

"I saw ye." She glanced up at him, then down at the cup he'd offered. Her trencher arrived just then, along with another cup. She picked up the new one.

Of course. She wasn't going to make it easy to get to know her. Her tone bordered on rudeness, but Tavish was willing to give her the benefit of the doubt to find out more about her.

"I ken ye are a stranger here. And ye are uncomfortable in a hall full of strange men. I apologize for waving at ye, but I thought to give ye a safe place to enjoy yer meal."

"Is not the entire keep a safe place?" She frowned as she asked the question, then attacked her trencher as if she hadn't eaten in a week.

Tavish approved of a lass with a hearty appetite.

"It is, aye. Normally. But with the gathering, there are many strangers here—"

She swallowed. "Are ye threatening me?"

"What? Nay. I'm protecting ye."

She shook her head. "I dinna need yer protection," she said and resumed eating.

"A lass alone in a strange hall—"

She sighed and rolled her eyes. "Just as I prefer to be. Please leave me."

It wasn't a request. Tavish knew that by her tone and the direct gaze she leveled on him. Those eyes! Brown and warm as sunlit pine bark, the very ones he'd gotten a glimpse of in his dream. And her hair—a bronze-shaded brown pulled into a loose plait and slung over her shoulder, full of tones that made him want to unravel it and hold each strand up to the sunlight. Its color would be deep and rich. Her skin was as smooth and fair as he'd seen in his vision.

How could he leave her alone in a hall full of strange men?

"What if I simply sit here and keep ye company while ye eat?"

In answer, she stood, picked up her trencher and cup and moved toward the stairs. Tavish frowned after her, not daring to glance toward the table where Bhaltair and his other companions still sat. Tavish got up and followed her, dodging laden serving lasses and other visitors who seemed determined to keep him from reaching her. "Let me help ye carry that," he suggested as he succeeded in getting within arm's reach. She was already on the stairs, a step above him.

She stopped her ascent and gave him a long look over her shoulder. "Ye didna understand me? Verra well, let me be clear. Leave me alone, or my da will make certain ye do."

"Who is yer da?" Brilliant. If she told him, he'd have no trouble keeping track of her.

"Keep this up," she said and twisted to meet his gaze, "and ye will find out. And ye willna like it."

With that, she turned and proceeded up the stairs, leaving Tavish nursing his wounded pride. He started up, but she glanced around and gave him a glare to boil his blood, so he stopped, conceding defeat—for now.

YVAINE REACHED THE TOP OF THE STAIRS AND GLANCED AROUND again to make sure that persistent man Tavish wasn't still following her. Who was he? Which laird did he serve? She must find out. If he continued to pester her, she might need to make good on her threat to tell her father.

He was rude, boorish, and arrogant to think she needed his help. Though he was rather good looking, she admitted. With dark auburn hair, he was tall and muscular, and had a pleasing, if somewhat overeager, countenance.

But nay, she was here to protect her Da, not meet the lads, no matter how well-favored their appearance might be.

He reminded her of Jamie Lathan, though he looked older than Jamie had when he fostered with them a few years back. Could he be another Lathan brother? The twin her da had not named? She reached her parent's door and knocked. In moments, her father opened it and gestured her in, then gave her a quizzical look, head tilted and eyebrows raised as he noticed what she carried. "Not much for the two of us," he commented softly. "Were ye too late today?"

"Nay," she replied after a glance to see her mother still asleep. "I had a persistent helper. I had to leave to get away from him. How is mother?"

"She woke up and ate some of what I brought her earlier, then fell asleep again. Ye stay here and eat. I'll go fetch another portion or two. Who's the lad ye had to leave behind?"

"Well, that's an interesting question. I thought about him on the way up and realized he reminds me of Jamie. He might be the other Lathan brother."

"Ye thought about him?"

"Well, he did annoy me," she answered drily as she moved to the chair her father had vacated, glad her back was to him. Her face might reveal her other thoughts about the man, as well. She set her food on the small table beside her.

Her father made a noise in his throat, then said, "He might be one of the twins. Tavish. I can see him, as one of the Lathan hosts, determined to look out for a lass alone. Especially one attractive enough to catch his eye."

"'Twasna like that, Da." She gave him a moue of disgust. "Dinna start pairing me with every new man we meet."

"Aye, lass. As ye say." He gave her a grin and exited before she could act on her sudden impulse to throw something at him—not that she would ever dare such disrespect.

Her mother stirred as the door closed. "A man who looks like Jamie?"

"Mother!" Yvaine set aside the cup she still held and reached for Ellie's hand as she sat up, then swung her legs off the side of the bed. "How are ye? Do ye need Da or the healer?"

"Nay. I feel...better. Hungry. Donal went to fetch more food?"

"Aye. Here—" Yvaine pushed the small table toward her mother. "Start on this. Da will be back soon."

Ellie sampled a little of everything, then tore off chunks of bread and dipped them in the meat juices in the bottom of the wooden platter. "This is just enough for now," she said after she swallowed. "Cider?"

"Aye." Yvaine handed her the cup. "Yer color is better. Ye look as though ye feel better."

"I do. Help me dress. I want to surprise Donal."

Yvaine leapt to assist her mother into a kirtle, then combed out her silver-streaked dark hair and braided it loosely to fall down her back. She'd always worn it long. Yvaine couldn't recall her ever cutting it, though had she not, it might trail the floor by now instead of being long enough to sit upon. "Ye look well. Da will be pleased."

"As am I, daughter. Thank ye."

The door opened just then and Donal backed in, then closed it with one foot and turned. He nearly dropped the trenchers he carried. "Ellie! My beautiful love. Ye look well," he exclaimed as he crossed the outer chamber and entered the bedchamber. He glanced around, helpless for a moment, until

Yvaine went to his rescue. "I'll take mine across the hall. She took a platter and a cup and left them to their joy.

Once she closed the door behind her, a sense of foreboding flared. What was it about hallways in this keep? She crossed to her chamber, but the feeling didn't fade as she entered. She set her food down on the chamber's small table and went to peer out the window. It was a lovely, sunny day, her mother had dressed, felt and looked much better, and her da was happy for that. What could be making her feel so unsettled?

Suddenly, she saw the man who'd tried to attach himself to her earlier in the great hall. Hadn't he said his name was Tavish? He seemed leaner than she remembered Jamie being the last time she'd seen him, but her memory could be playing tricks on her. Jamie had left battle-worn and angry, grieving for a dead friend and blaming her da for the loss. Why would Tavish cause her unease? Did it mean he held a grudge for Jamie's sake over the way he'd left MacKyrie?

Tavish didn't bother to return to the table where Bhaltair and the others were finishing their meal. He was in no mood to relate what had happened with the lass, then have to listen to their advice on what he should have done, or worse, put up with their laughter.

Instead, he made his way across the great hall and down the hallway that led past the kitchen toward his mother's herbal. She might have an idea who the lass was.

How could his dream lass be such a spoiled brat? Of all the things he had imagined about her during the weeks she had lived in his visions, he had never expected to dislike her. But the fact remained that she had appeared, and his visions portended...something. He needed to know more.

Damn, why did he behave the way he did? The strange lass

didn't know his visions made him fear she could be in danger, and if so, he would do all he could to keep her safe. He'd just run her off, and made her think he was a man she should avoid. Maybe that was why she'd behaved the way she did.

Even worse, if she was a source of danger to those he loved, he'd just ruined his chance to stay close to her and discover what she planned.

At least she'd gone upstairs. He presumed she had a chamber there—with her parents? She warned him her Da would take care of him. He was no saint, but she was the first lass he couldn't get out of his mind. Others had caught his interest and even welcomed him into their beds, but only this one inhabited his dreams and visions. She couldn't be taken from him before he even knew who she was! But the sense of foreboding in his visions told him it was possible.

He entered the herbal, glad to see his twin, Eilidh, was there with their mother. Judging by the number of strangers in the great hall, his earlier admonition to her was well delivered. All the Lathans would be wise to keep an eye on the lasses in the Lathan stronghold. There could be more dangers inside their gates than one older laird with a penchant for younger lasses. Eilidh was not the only one who would attract a great deal of male attention. His dream lass had certainly captured his, and she would garner more from any man who saw her.

From the smells he'd noted wafting out the door of the herbal, he could tell they were concocting another poultice. He recognized the scent of the most common ingredient, meadow sweet. A basket of sphagnum moss sat on a nearby table, and the sun shone through the open door that led outside to the walled garden, bringing in fresh air and accounting for the scents reaching the inner hallway.

"Are ye expecting a battlefield's worth of wounds to treat?" He kept his tone light, but the question was serious.

Eilidh snorted, but their mother answered. "With strangers

here and in the glen, ye ken fine 'tis prudent to prepare more than we would normally keep on hand. Ye can use these on minor wounds while Eilidh and I care for the more seriously injured."

"Ye truly expect there to be some? Those men are here for a gathering about a peace treaty, not to settle a feud."

With so many people depending on Lathan hospitality, Aileana took seriously making her herbal ready for anything. She was a Healer, not a Seer, but she had years of experience and knew large gatherings often led to accidents, or fights, or injuries sustained during a hunt, or worse, so she didn't surprise Tavish when she replied, "I hope there will not be any violence, but 'tis possible. Even likely."

Tavish inspected the contents of the steaming pot without comment.

"Has everyone arrived, or do I need to go back out to the gate with ye?" Eilidh didn't look eager to resume the duty their father had given them.

"When I came in, only one laird was still missing. We dinna need to go back out there." Tavish frowned. "But that is not why I came. Have either of ye seen a lass who would have arrived with a laird in the last day? This tall." He held up a hand at his eye level, then dropped it. "Brown hair."

"And quite pretty, too, of course? She's here?" Eilidh shook her head at her brother's narrowed eyes. Her voice had betrayed her excitement, pitching a little higher than her usual timbre. Then she collected herself. "Nay, I havena seen anyone like that. But I was out with ye and then in here the rest of the morning."

Aileana quirked her lip at her daughter, then glanced sharply his way. "Why do ye ask?"

Before he could answer, a lad appeared in the herbal's doorway. "Ach, there ye are. Tavish, the laird wants ye in his solar."

4

By mid-afternoon, Kilgore had made a base for himself at the edge of the glen's tent encampment. Satisfied, he stalked into the trees, looking for a vantage point that let him watch the activity there while he also kept an eye on the path up to the Aerie's gates. His fists clenched and brow drawn down into a frustrated frown, he climbed and finally found a place on the glen's sloping side close to the tor, where he could do both. He needed to find a way into the Aerie that didn't draw attention to himself from the gate guards. Failing that, he needed to find a way to draw his target out of the keep and down into the glen. So far, none of the men in the glen had ventured up the steep trail that led to the Aerie's gates. He'd sought this place to separate himself from the rest of the lairds' entourages because the longer he waited in the encampment in the glen, the more concerned he became that someone would recognize him or question which laird he served, and his chance to avenge the wrong done to his clan would be taken from him.

But perhaps his luck had just changed. A group of men was gathering, and if they intended to climb the tor for the evening meal, they would pass directly by him.

He could join them and enter the keep unnoticed in the crowd.

He bided his time, fingering the hilt of the dirk in his belt, and fighting the urge to reach down and reassure himself his *sgian dubh* was still in his boot. He knew it was. He was never without either of these blades. They had been handed down to him from his grandfather, the MacDuff laird Donal MacNabb killed more than twenty years ago when Kilgore was just a lad. His father had told him the tale. Kilgore's thirst for vengeance had burned until he'd grown into a man strong enough to bury one or both of his blades in MacNabb's heart. It should have been done before now. His da had been a weak excuse of a man, and had done nothing save bow to their new laird—a lass —and do his best to escape notice.

Kilgore swore. He was no coward. Now that he was old enough and skilled enough to take on the great Donal MacNabb, it was his turn. He was stronger and smarter than his father had ever dreamed of being. He would restore honor to his line. If he could accomplish that and remain unseen, so much the better. He would preserve his future and reclaim his rightful inheritance, and his clan's true name—MacDuff.

TAVISH ENTERED THE LAIRD'S SOLAR BEHIND HIS BROTHER Drummond, not surprised to see Bhaltair already there.

Bhaltair nodded as they took seats. "Blame me, lads," he said. "Ye need to ken this before the gathering begins in the morning."

Toran leaned back in his chair, then apparently thought better of it and sat forward, resting his elbows on his desk, and nodded to Bhaltair. "Now that we're all here, what do ye have to tell us?"

"I'm already hearing rumblings of trouble in the encampment in the glen," Bhaltair began.

Toran frowned. "So soon? Rumblings, ye say."

"Aye. No real violence as yet, but 'tis likely."

"What else should I ken before I meet with the lairds? Why is this happening?"

Bhaltair pressed his lips into a thin line, then spoke. "Clan rivalries that should have been set aside by the treaty, and especially should not have continued past a clan's signing. Some rash talk and a few minor fist fights among the men. 'Tis likely to get worse."

"Has anyone heard of such among the visiting lairds?"

"Nay," Bhaltair answered.

"'Tis good that there are no women in the camp," Drummond said. "I believe only two lairds' wives came with their husbands, and they bide with them inside the Aerie's gates. The men will be easier to control without the complication of lasses adding to the tensions in the glen."

"I suggest restricting all women and bairns—even our own —to the keep unless escorted," Bhaltair continued. "If tensions continue to mount, a woman's presence could spark trouble. As of yet, there's been no blood spilled."

Toran frowned. "I will warn the lairds on pain of expulsion to keep their people civil and in control." He looked from Drummond to Tavish. "Keep yer eyes and ears open, and report anything that bodes troublesome to Bhaltair or me."

Tavish's belly tightened. He hadn't mentioned his visions to anyone yet, save his twin sister. As far as he knew, they did not necessarily mean much of anything, but now the lass was here.

He'd only followed her in the dreams, nay more. There seemed to be no one else in them. Still, they gave him an uneasy feeling. Tavish had not seen the reason why the lass appeared in his vision or precisely where their encounters took place. The dream's surroundings didn't help. Stone was widely used everywhere in the keep, and his focus stayed so tightly on the lass that when she appeared, all else receded into darkness. He couldn't even say what sparked his unease.

If he mentioned her, if he warned his father while knowing no more than he knew right now, Toran would be frustrated by his vague forebodings. To be able to take action, the laird would require more information, and so far, Tavish had nothing more to tell him other than the fact that the lass was no longer in his dreams. She now walked about in the keep.

Bhaltair would put every Lathan warrior on high alert. They were already, but Bhaltair would find a way to ensure even greater vigilance. And the lass in question, no matter who the father was that she'd threatened him with, whoever she was, would find herself confined to her chamber until time to return home. Tavish risked causing trouble with her clan over dreams. Worrisome dreams, aye, but dreams lacking specificity. He must wait.

He hoped he would not regret that decision.

YVAINE ANSWERED A KNOCK ON HER DOOR ONLY AFTER SHE HEARD a feminine voice on the other side call out to her. A lass stood in the hall who could only be a Lathan. She was blessed with the similar height, features, thick auburn hair and air of energy, though muted, as Jamie, the only Lathan sibling Yvaine knew. Or knew well. The lad who'd driven her from the great hall could be another Lathan.

"I'm Eilidh," she said. "Ye must be Yvaine. The steward told me the MacKyrie laird brought a lass with her, along with her husband, Donal MacNabb. But the steward didna say ye were of an age with me. I expected to find a lass I might take to the nursery to meet the other bairns."

Yvaine didn't know where to start to reply to Eilidh's greeting. After a breath, she decided to take her comments in order. "I am Yvaine. Come in," she offered and stepped to the side.

Eilidh stepped in at her gesture and settled on the hearthside chair, leaving the bed as Yvaine's only other option for seating.

"I'm sorry if my age disappoints ye—"

"Ach, nay," Eilidh said, cutting off her apology. "I'm glad to meet a lass of an age to be a friend. There are few enough of those in the Aerie." She paused and looked aside, then said, "Sorry, I hope I dinna presume. I talk too much when I'm nervous."

"About being friends? Nay, our families are allied, so of course, 'tis possible."

That seemed to satisfy Eilidh. She gave a single nod.

"And my da used to be the arms master here," Yvaine said to fill the silence. "He says we're family."

Eilidh tipped her head to the side as if thinking it over. "Aye. I've heard my da say the same. Yer da fostered here with my grandda, and he trained my da, the laird, and most of our warriors. So, we are cousins of a sort."

Yvaine relaxed at Eilidh's words. She'd been accepted. "Cousins, then. I'm glad." She spread her hands. "I dinna have any of those nearby MacKyrie. After Flodden, my mother was left an only child, and my da hasna been back to MacNabb in ages. Most of his life. If I've any cousins there, I've never met them."

"'Tis sad we have that in common," Eilidh said. "My mother's half-brother died trying to save her from the invaders who brought her here, and my da's brother died at Flodden. So, I have none I ken about, either." Eilidh paused as if searching for something else to say. "Would ye like to see some of the Aerie?"

"I would," Yvaine told her. "I've heard a great deal about it from my da."

A frown creased Eilidh's brow, but it fled quickly. "Come with me, then. I'll show ye around."

Yvaine couldn't help but wonder at the frown, but once Eilidh led her down the stairs, she noticed only the looks they got from the men hanging about the great hall as they passed through. The curiosity on most faces, she could accept. But the intense interest worried her, and the hunger in a few eyes made her belly clench. But she dismissed them since Eilidh seemed to pay them no mind. Yvaine assumed that since she accompanied the laird's youngest daughter in her own keep, they'd be safe.

Eilidh showed Yvaine the buttery, introduced her to the weavers, one of whom, Yvaine was surprised to learn, had recently married the Lathan heir. They chatted with her long enough to get the bare bones of her story, then moved on past the smithy to the stable. "We've a family of late pups in here," Eilidh told her. "Six weeks old," she added as she led Yvaine to one of the stalls. Inside, a mutt of indeterminate mixture sat with five puppies playing around her.

"I love wee animals," Yvaine said and entered. "But will she permit..." She leaned her head toward the mother.

"Aye. She's used to all the bairns coming in here to visit. We're much calmer than they are. She'll appreciate that."

Reassured, Yvaine knelt and let the round-bellied puppies' natural curiosity draw them, bouncing and teetering on their too-large paws, to climb onto her lap. All but one. It stumbled and collapsed halfway there. Yvaine immediately knew something was wrong. She stretched out a hand and picked up the wee pup. It struggled for breath as its tongue lolled out one side of its mouth.

"What have ye gotten into, laddie?" She checked its nose and opened its mouth, gently pulling its tongue out of the way to see into its throat. "Ach, nay." With gentle fingers, she probed and tugged out a piece of straw matted with fur, then she rubbed his wee belly until he took a clear breath. "There ye go, wee man. Ye are too young to swallow such as that."

"How did he?"

"Likely he found it stuck in his ma's fur beside the teat he favors, and he swallowed it before he realized he was in the wrong spot."

"Ye saved him."

"This time." She held up the pup and looked him over. He was breathing normally and squirming in her hands. "Ye must take care, wee one," she advised, stroked his head with one finger, then reached out to put him on the ground closer to his dam. He waddled to her as Yvaine brushed her hands on her skirt.

"Ye should meet my sister Lianna," Eilidh told her. "Ye seem to have her way with animals."

"I'd like that," Yvaine told her as she picked up the first of the squirming pups to come to her. It rewarded her with a lick on her cheek. "These are adorable. Who will train them?" She petted the one she held, then rubbed the soft ears of another that climbed into her lap.

"That depends on what they'll do."

"I see them herding sheep, and cattle, too."

"My twin brother said much the same. They'll be too small to be hunting dogs."

"It must be wonderful to have a twin," Yvaine said as she put down the first pup and picked up the second and the next to climb into her lap.

Eilidh snorted. "I wouldna call it wonderful. All of my brothers can be overprotective, even Tavish, but the eldest, Drummond, is the worst. Or he was. He's married now, with a young son."

"That should distract him," Yvaine said in agreement, then

one of Eilidh's words finally registered. *Tavish*. "Yer twin's name is Tavish?"

"Aye. Have ye met him? Looks like me, but taller…"

Yvaine's expression must have registered because she trailed off.

"I believe so. There was a man in the great hall who seemed determined to become my companion. My escort. I had to return to my chamber to escape him."

"That sounds like my twin," Eilidh said and snorted. "He means well. Truly he does."

Yvaine put the pups down and stood, careful not to step on any tiny paws or tails. She should have recognized the resemblance as soon as she opened her door to Eilidh. "Did he send ye to keep watch over me?"

"Nay, no one sent me. I told ye—"

Yvaine nodded. Of course, she would say that. "I think I'd best go back upstairs. I should check on my mother."

"My mother has been helping her. I, too."

"Ye are a healer?"

"I am. Someday I will take over for my mother as the Lathan healer, but I have many years to train before that will happen."

Yvaine gave her a tight smile. "I hope so. Now, if ye will excuse me…"

"Ach, nay, 'tis best I go with ye, at least through the great hall. 'Tis full of strange men. A lass alone might not be safe."

"And two are better?" The looks they'd gotten while crossing the great hall returned to her in a rush.

"Aye. If they bother us, we can fight together until Bhaltair and his men arrive."

"Bhaltair?"

"Lathan's chief guard. Ye canna miss him. He's one of the biggest men in the keep, but *dinna fash*. He looks fierce, but he'd never harm a lass." She held a hand well above her head, her

eyes sparkling and making Yvaine wonder if there was something between them.

"It seems I have many protective new people to meet," she
said. And if all of them were as persistent as the Lathan twins,
she might never have a moment to herself.

5

T avish and Drummond entered the great hall together. From the crowd, Tavish presumed most of the lairds had arrived in time for supper. If all had gone according to plan, they were residing in chambers in one of the Aerie's towers, and their men stayed in tents in the glen, though many climbed the tor for their meals rather than live on travel rations they'd brought with them.

Their mother sat at one of the nearby tables, talking to a striking couple. The laird was a large man. He would rival Bhaltair in size, or so Tavish guessed. He wouldn't be sure until the man stood up. The woman with him had long, silver-streaked black hair she wore loose, and striking features. She might be tall for a woman, he couldn't tell, but he was certain she would never rival her husband in size.

Drummond grabbed Tavish's arm, stopping his forward momentum. "See that couple sitting with mother—do ye recognize them?"

"Nay. Do ye?"

"Nay, but I think I ken who they might be. If I'm right, I want to meet them."

They approached the table from an angle that let Aileana see them coming. She smiled and waved them forward. "Ah, good. I'm glad ye are here. Donal, Ellie, these are two of my lads. Drummond is the heir, and Tavish is the twin I want ye to talk to, Ellie."

Donal stood, allowing Tavish to take his full measure. Bhaltair still topped him by an inch or two, but Donal's size was impressive. And this was Ellie, the MacKyrie Seer, whom he hoped would help him with his own talent.

"I'm pleased to meet both of ye," Drummond said and gave the Seer a slight bow.

"As am I," Tavish added.

Ellie turned her attention to Tavish, and studied him.

Tavish held himself still, not knowing how far her senses extended.

"Sit with us," Donal said. "I havena seen Drummond since ye were a wee bairn. The MacKyrie glen is too far away to allow frequent visits."

Ellie laughed. "Anything would be frequent against a twenty-year gap, husband."

"Indeed, wife," Donal replied and gave her a grin. Tavish was struck by his light green eyes. On another man, they would appear cold and off-putting, but Donal seemed comfortable and even friendly, at least when in the company of his wife. This was the man his older brother Jamie had fought with, blaming him for the death of a dear friend in battle, then leaving MacKyrie with bad feelings? It didn't seem possible.

Drummond took a seat at their mother's side and began questioning the MacKyrie couple about life in their glen, their whisky business and whether the treaty had put an end to trouble with their neighbors.

"Less the treaty, I think," Ellie said, "than my marriage to Donal. It stymied the ambitions of those lairds who thought to acquire MacKyrie through marriage to me. And the treaty gave us defenders sufficient to discourage any who intended to invade us. None have tried to disturb that arrangement. Though, possibly now..."

Aye, she was the laird, Tavish recalled, as well as a Seer. Before he could ask what she meant by "possibly now," Drummond spoke up.

"Who holds MacKyrie for ye while ye are here?"

Drummond's question was an excellent one. Tavish wondered how a woman could be laird and be strong enough to protect her clan.

"Our son, Micheil," Donal answered. "And his namesake, Ellie's life-long, closest friend, to support him. MacKyrie is much stronger than it was when Ellie and I first met. The lads have grown up—"

"And ye trained them to be formidable warriors," Ellie said, interrupting him.

"Aye, and from the treaty clans, we gained men to fight, and men with skills we sorely needed, as Ellie said. Some stayed long enough to train replacements, some married and remain with us to this day."

Donal seemed quite satisfied with the way events had gone at MacKyrie.

"Did ye bring any of yer whisky with ye?"

If Drummond had been in reach, Tavish would have elbowed him for that question. But Ellie seemed not to take offense.

"Aye, we did. A gift for Laird Lathan. Ye will have to appeal to him."

Aileana laughed.

"Or come to MacKyrie," Ellie continued, shifting her gaze to Tavish. "I understand ye would like some help with yer talent."

"I would," Tavish admitted. "As ye have time. Da has planned for much to discuss over the next few days."

"I will make time," Ellie promised with a smile. Then she

turned to Aileana. "Perhaps tomorrow. If ye dinna mind, I believe I will check on Yvaine, who is resting, and then retire. Donal, if ye will see me upstairs, ye dinna need to stay with me. I'm sure ye and Toran have much to discuss."

Tavish and Drummond stood as she rose. Donal escorted her away. Aileana's gaze followed them. "I think she can help ye, Tavish, but mayhap it will take another day or two. Until she feels strong enough."

"Are ye caring for her?"

"Aye. A female complaint. Not as serious as some, but painful. She has borne it far too long."

"So ye take her pain," Drummond remarked with a frown.

"For a wee time. And for the good of all of us. Ellie is a treasure we canna do without. Now, lads, I believe I will also go to my rest. Yer da is in his solar, and Donal will join him soon. They might even open that cask of whisky." She smiled and left them.

"Go on, if ye wish," Tavish told Drummond. "There's aught else I want to do."

Drummond grinned and headed for the laird's solar.

———

Yvaine heard her parents come upstairs, then heard her father leave again. Her mother probably intended to rest, but Yvaine wanted to check on her first, then she'd let her sleep.

She slipped across the hall and knocked on the door. "Mother?"

"Coming." In moments, the door opened and Ellie stood there. She looked much better. Tired, but the pinched skin around her eyes had smoothed.

"I just wanted to make certain ye were well."

"I am better, but tired. How are ye, daughter?" She gestured Yvaine inside, and they went to the chairs in front of the hearth.

"Better, too. I ate my supper from the tray ye sent up. Thank ye for that."

"Travel is tiring. Ye will feel more yerself tomorrow."

"As will ye, I hope."

"Aye. Aileana will see to it. I met the heir, Drummond, and one of the younger twins, Tavish, downstairs. The resemblance between all the brothers is uncanny."

"The sisters, too, I think. I met Eilidh today. She came to my chamber, then showed me some of the keep."

"No wonder ye were tired," Ellie said, then continued as if Yvaine hadn't spoken. "Drummond is married, but Tavish is still unwed. And quite handsome."

"Mother..." It seemed she couldn't go anywhere or speak to anyone without his name coming up.

Ellie laughed. "I canna help wanting to see ye happy, daughter."

"I am happy. Save for the dreams that have made me fear for Da. Ye still havena had a seeing?" After her mother shook her head, Yvaine continued, "I'll be glad when ye no longer need the tisane. Perhaps ye will see more than I have been able to."

"I will do without it this night and going forward. Aileana has relieved the pain."

"I'm glad." Yvaine stood. "Get some sleep, Mother."

"Ye, too, Daughter. I will see ye in the morning."

Yvaine kissed her cheek and left. She was too restless to sleep yet. Her chamber's window drew her to look out over the bailey. She breathed in the cool night air, grateful for the opening that kept her chamber from feeling closed in. She thrived in the open air of the MacKyrie's wide and long glen. The idea of being confined, unable to free herself, made her shudder.

She knew why she felt that way. She'd heard the story of her parent's romance, but the story had a darker side, too. The former MacDuff laird had invaded and threatened her mother's people to force her mother to marry him. With the help of the defrocked priest who made their whisky, her mother had ensured the marriage was not valid. Yvaine had known that much all her life. But only recently had she found out he'd been intent on bedding her by force, beating her until she was powerless to protect herself. Donal MacNabb snuck into the keep with his men and defeated the MacDuff invaders. To deal with the disturbance, MacDuff had left her mother before he finished assaulting her. Donal had killed the MacDuff laird, saved her mother from a horrible fate, and they'd lived happily ever after. But the images that filled her mind of what her mother suffered—and nearly suffered—at MacDuff's hands were enough to make Yvaine fear being overpowered and locked up with no means of escape. Her father could not know how his threat to lock her in her chamber for her own safety stole her breath. And she couldn't tell him. He would be appalled at himself for frightening her, and concerned for her.

She wrapped her arms around herself and forced her attention back to the cool night air and the bailey.

It wasn't late enough for everyone to seek their beds. A few people moved around down there and snippets of conversation reached her. Two lads led a late arrival's horse into the stable. A couple walked hand-in-hand, enjoying the clear evening, and talking softly. She couldn't hear what they said, but their loving voices carried to her at her window. They paused and the man looked at the lass with such devotion Yvaine lifted her hand to her heart.

Would she ever have a love like that?

Her father seemed to think she might meet someone here. And her mother mentioned Tavish Lathan. She wasn't sure what to make of that. Her mother had never tried to make a match for her. But she was an excellent judge of people. And that confused Yvaine. What she had seen of Tavish so far did not fit with her mother's favorable assessment. He'd annoyed her from the moment they met, trying to convince her she needed him to keep her safe. Did he not know she was Donal MacNabb's daughter? She could take care of herself. Any man she fell in love with would have to respect her abilities, her independence, and her wishes, just as her father respected and loved her mother.

By the time Yvaine turned her attention again to the bailey, the couple moved on beyond her view. But the full moon was rising behind the eastern peaks. Yvaine liked looking at it. She believed everyone in the world saw the same moon and it made her feel connected to people she missed, like her brother, Michiel, and even to people she'd never met, in the Highlands and beyond.

Her time would come. Her parents would never force her to marry against her will. She could be certain of a love match. But first, she had to meet a man worth falling in love with.

That man was not Tavish Lathan.

TAVISH LEFT THE GREAT HALL. BEFORE HE WENT TO HIS REST, HE wanted to see if he could find the place his visions had shown him. Now that he knew the lass in them was real, finding the location of the visions took on greater urgency.

If he could identify at least that much, he could post guards there. Or if he found out who she was, he could keep her away from it until his dreams showed him what was going to happen. The keep and its towers occupied much of the top of the tor inside the defensive walls, but there were also other buildings like the stables, the weavers' chambers, the washhouse, the smithy, the buttery, the wee kirk, and more. Between and around them were hides and closes used to hang laundry, store empty barrels, firewood, and other odds and ends that were part of life in a keep.

His search took him away from the gates, deeper in to the bailey. Nothing seemed to match exactly what he'd seen. It was getting too dark to be certain, and the light from the torches on the battlements did not reach this far. One stone wall looked much like another in the gloom. Frustrated, he decided to return to the great hall.

He came around the corner of the south tower in time to see someone trailing Donal MacNabb toward the stable. After taking his wife to their chamber, Donal must have decided to check on the MacKyrie mounts before joining Toran in the laird's solar. Tavish paused and watched for a moment. Something about the way the other man moved told Tavish he was up to no good.

Spurred by concern for his father's old friend, Tavish caught up with the stranger and put a hand on his shoulder.

The man spun, brandishing a dirk in his fist, menacing Tavish while Donal walked on, unaware of his peril, and disappeared into the stable.

"Easy, friend," Tavish said, holding up his hands and keeping them away from the blade in his own belt. "Ye shouldna be in this part of the keep. Are ye lost?"

"It seems so. I just came up from the glen. I'm looking for my supper."

"The evening meal is in the great hall." The man should have known that. His excuse was thin.

He sheathed his blade, dropped his shoulders and nodded. "Aye, then I suppose I am lost. I thought to follow someone, expecting they'd be headed for their meal, too, but I must have picked the wrong man." His gaze shifted toward the stable and for the briefest of moments, it hardened and hatred blazed in his eyes, then he blinked and the heat disappeared, replaced by earnestness.

He wanted Tavish to believe him. The raised hairs on the back of Tavish's neck convinced him of what the man's amiable tone sought to hide. He wasn't lost. And he hadn't picked the wrong man. He had been following Donal. Tavish was glad he'd come by when he did. Donal could take care of himself as well or better than any man save, possibly, Bhaltair. But no man was immune to a blade in the back.

"Let me show ye to the great hall." Tavish gestured for the man to accompany him, and stepped aside. No way was he going to let this man walk behind him. He was no fool. "I'm Tavish Lathan. And ye are?"

"Kilgore," he said.

Tavish had no proof, other than the unease in his belly, both that Donal had been in danger, and that the man was lying to him now about his name. Was this part of his talent? Could a Seer sense wrongness even if it wasn't in a vision? He'd have to ask Ellie MacKyrie when she was able to speak with him.

In the meantime, unlike his dreams about the lass, this he had seen with his own eyes and this he would report. They reached the great hall and the man thanked him and sank into a seat at a trestle table as a serving lass came by with a tray of cups of ale. Tavish left him there and went to the solar.

Both Toran and Bhaltair were still there. They looked up as he entered. "Da? Ye need to hear what just happened." He waved Bhaltair back to his seat when he stood to give them privacy. "Ye, too." Then he related what he'd just seen and done. "Kilgore should still be out there, Bhaltair, if ye want to take a look." He described the man and what he was wearing.

Bhaltair nodded and left the solar.

"Following Donal." Toran's eyes held storm clouds. "Ye did right to keep the man unaware of yer suspicions. We'll watch him. If he's here to kill Donal, he'll not get another chance."

Tavish let out a sigh of relief. Maybe his dreams were only

dreams after all, and the foreboding he'd sensed had more to do with Donal MacNabb. Perhaps the attractive lass was only a symbol for a coming danger, a symbol he was sure to pay attention to. Now that Bhaltair and his father were aware the threat to Donal appeared to be real, Tavish didn't have to carry that burden alone. Donal should arrive in moments from the stables, and Bhaltair would make him aware of the man who'd followed him.

Tavish would watch and wait a while longer before he mentioned the lass to anyone. He'd yet to learn her name, and he'd seen no threat directed at her. But what then was her connection to Donal? There must be a reason he had dreamt of her and not of him.

6

T he next day, Tavish joined his father and brother in the laird's gathering. Though he wasn't the heir, if anything happened to Drummond in the future, that duty would fall to him. Jamie, the youngest triplet, two years Tavish's senior, had married away from the clan and chosen to pursue his healing talent rather than acting as the spare for clan Lathan. Though that was not necessarily Jamie's permanent future plan, it served for the moment to put Tavish in the position of supporting the heir.

Given that, he needed to meet the other lairds and become known to them. But he never expected to take on the mantle of laird. Their father was still strong and young, and they expected Drummond would not replace him for many more years. Given Drummond's recent marriage, he could soon have an heir of his own, and both Jamie and Tavish would no longer be in line to take over Clan Lathan. Tavish knew he was not suited to the job. His talent made him too prone to thinking rather than acting, and his rare visions during daytime would be deadly, should one occur in the heat of battle.

Nonetheless, he trained—carefully—and prepared for what

he considered the worst that could happen, even as he struggled to master his talent. He couldn't control it, but he needed
to. Soon after his voice changed and the visions started, he'd
been caught up in a vision during training. His partner had not
noticed his sudden thrall until just before smashing his head in
with a wooden practice sword, and had managed to turn his
blow aside. Since then, Tavish had trained with Drummond or
Bhaltair, plus one or two others who knew what to look for if he
became lost in a seeing. It had happened only a handful of
times since then. The older he got, the more his visions came
during sleep, sometimes powerful and overwhelming, crisp,
clear, and brief. And sometimes, like the visions of the lass,
they remained vague and disturbing. All he could do was
surrender to their power and try to make sense of what he saw.

The gathered lairds barely fit in Toran's solar. Eleven lairds,
twelve with their host, the Lathan laird, had signed the treaty
Toran developed after the battle of Flodden took the lives of his
father and older brother, as well as those of the lairds sitting
here today. He conceived of the idea that the remaining
battered and weakened clans, many of which had lost most of
their fighting men, must band together to protect each other
against incursions by not only the English, but Lowlander
Scots and possibly other Highland clans as well. Most, but not
all, of the nearby clans had joined the treaty and remained
allied to this day. Two were missing from the gathering,
including Tavish's sister Lianna's husband, but had sent
missives stating their support of the Lathan laird.

Adding to the crowding in the chamber, each laird brought
a guard or assistant to fetch and carry and to guard their principal's back. These men were allied with Lathan and each other,
but they were not foolish. In a group this size, disagreements
were inevitable, and tempers could flare. The only laird not
flaunting a bodyguard was Toran, but with Drummond at his
side, he was as well protected as any of the visitors. Tavish's

presence in the chamber added another layer of security. But Toran was even better protected than many of the attending lairds knew.

Tavish listened while Toran went through his plans for the gathering. The King, James V, had taken control of the lawless border with England several years before. For the most part, he left it to the lairds to control the northern reaches as long as their actions didn't undermine his rule—and their nobles paid the taxes he demanded of them and of the kirk. Everyone knew the King wandered the countryside as a peasant, seeking commoner opinions of his rule. But Toran announced that rumors had reached the Highlands that his tactics would soon change, and he would soon assert his dominance over not just the Northern and Western isles, but much of the Highlands, as well. How this would affect the treaty and its member clans' relations outside of it was a matter of great concern. The King adhered to the Auld Alliance with France, and had recently married his second French wife, Marie de Guise. But his uncle, Henry VIII, supported the Reformation, fomenting religious unrest in Scotland, which could eventually reach the treaty clans. It was an impressive set of concerns.

Tavish studied the men while his father began the day's discussion. He knew the MacAnalen laird, of course, their closest neighbor and ally, at whose village Toran had been taken captive by an invading lowlander army and met Tavish's mother, the healer. Formidable Donal MacNabb sat in for his wife and laird, Ellie MacKyrie, whom Aileana treated for some women's complaint. Jamie Lathan, Toran's cousin and oldest friend, had arrived late last night and attended for his wife, the Fletcher laird. With those three in the chamber, Toran had men who considered themselves not just allies, but family. They made up a strong contingent fully with him should any discussion begin to veer from the path he intended to set—or any violence erupt.

Tavish turned his attention to the secondary members of the gathering. Most, by their relaxed watchfulness as they stood with their backs to the wall behind their principals, were clearly guards. Others came and went as their principal directed, fetching ale or anything else needed. Tavish dismissed them as inconsequential until a new face entered the chamber and took up position along the wall in the gap behind the MacThomas and MacBean lairds.

Tavish recognized him immediately as Kilgore, the man who'd followed Donal MacNabb. Even if he hadn't known him, the man's gaze tracking immediately to Donal would have reminded Tavish who he was. With his gaze on his quarry, Kilgore's demeanor changed. He tensed and his hands flexed at his side. One landed on the hilt of his dirk and stayed there. Then his gaze left Donal and slid around the room.

Tavish held his ground. There was nowhere to hide, and no reason not to confront Kilgore if he offered a threat. But Tavish didn't like his hand on his dirk, even if rested there only out of habit.

The man caught Tavish's eye and his gaze grew cold. In response, Tavish quirked his lips and inclined his head as if to say, *aye, I do ken ye and I'm watching ye.* The man ripped his gaze away and stared over the heads of the lairds seated before him to the wall behind Toran's head. If Kilgore was here to cause the kind of trouble Tavish suspected of him, he'd been warned that he could not do anything without being observed.

———

Yvaine escorted her mother to the great hall for a meal after she woke up from the healer's earlier session with her. She seemed even better than she had last evening.

"I'm grateful for Aileana's care, of course," Ellie said, "but

I'm glad to leave our chamber and see new faces. I've seen little of the keep since we arrived."

"Would ye like to walk in the bailey before we eat? 'Tis a lovely day out of doors."

"Later, perhaps. I find I'm most hungry."

"I, too." Her mother's words lightened Yvaine's mood. Ellie's hunger was a clear sign that whatever Aileana was doing for her was working. Yvaine found a pair of seats well away from other people where they could sit and watchthe comings and goings through the great hall while they ate.

"Perfect," Ellie observed as she seated herself. "Close enough to see everyone, but far enough to speak privately."

Yvaine signaled to a serving lass, then turned to her mother. "Privately? Do we need to discuss something?"

"Aye, daughter. Now that I'm feeling better, I can see that we need to discuss yer visions. Something has ye on edge. Ye talked yer da into letting ye come with us, and though I ken ye offered to help me, there's more to this, aye? Ye are worried about him and have asked several times whether I have had any visions. Tell me what ye have seen."

Yvaine waited until their food had been placed before them and cups of cider provided before she answered. "Not much, truly. A few symbols, like ye often see. But I have been plagued with a sense of foreboding. Of danger."

"Toward Donal?"

"Aye, toward Da, I think. I dinna ken why, but I feel he is under threat."

"I've seen nothing to confirm that."

"Nay, but ye have been taking a sleeping draught for weeks. Does it not suppress yer visions?"

Ellie huffed out a sigh. "Aye, it does. And perhaps at the very worst time. 'Tis good that ye have some ability to warn us. Still, now that Aileana has begun to help me, I no longer need to rely on a potion to sleep. Perhaps soon I will see what has been hidden from ye." She paused to take a sip of cider, then continued. "Or perhaps there is nothing to see." She broke off a piece of bread and studied it. "Some dreams are just dreams," she said and popped the bit of bread into her mouth. After she chewed and swallowed, she added, "Even if they are bad dreams. Worrisome dreams. Some feelings come from nowhere and return whence they came, too, signifying naught, save perhaps an uncomfortable belly. Perhaps what ye have sensed is nay more than that."

Yvaine watched her mother eat. It eased some of her fears to see this sign of improvement. She took a bite from her own trencher, then replied. "Perhaps," she said, then shook her head. "But it has stayed with me for long enough that I canna discount it. I have hoped for a clear vision. All I've seen are vague indications of the danger—a blade or shadows, but thus far, 'tis mostly a hollowness in my belly. A feeling that makes the hair stand up on my neck. A not-quite fear that disturbs my sleep, but shows me naught."

Ellie reached over and patted her hand. "I am sorry. Still, perhaps these feelings, the uneasiness, come only from being a lass."

"Mother, I'm near to one-and-twenty. I should be long past all of that."

"Or perhaps this is a phase in your development as a Seer," Ellie told her. "Yer talent has never been strong, but perhaps it is about to change, to strengthen. There was a time when I thought mine had faded away, only to have it come back clearer and sharper than ever."

"Then let that be soon," Yvaine told her, "So that if Da is in danger, I will see the source before it is too late. Or ye will."

"Here comes yer da now," Ellie said. "Ye have told him?"

"Aye, of course." She glanced aside to watch him approach and her heart swelled with love and affection. He was her rock. He'd trained her to protect herself and spent more time with her than any of the rest of her family. She could not think of losing him. She would not. "He needs to ken..."

"I agree, *dinna fash*." She made room for her husband to sit by her as she smiled up at him and said, "For now, I wish to hear what ye discussed in the morning's gathering."

Movement near the entrance to the laird's solar caught Yvaine's eye. Tavish entered the great hall and looked around, his gaze searching. Was he looking for her? She looked away, but couldn't help watching him from beneath lowered lashes as she pretended to listen to her parents' conversation. He moved with strength and a fighter's grace that she found herself admiring, and even more surprising, enjoying. Still, she tensed as he passed behind her and her parents, but he kept going and found a seat on the other side of the hall. As he crossed, people greeted him, and he acknowledged each of them. Surely he couldn't be as annoying to everyone as he'd been to her, or he wouldn't be so well regarded by the people of his clan. Had she been wrong about him?

WHEN THE MORNING SESSION BROKE UP, EVERYONE FILED OUT OF the solar for the midday meal. All save Toran, Drummond, and Tavish.

"What did ye see, lad?" Toran asked him.

His father didn't miss much. He must have noticed the exchange with Kilgore. "I think we have a problem. Did ye see the man standing behind the MacThomas laird? He's the one I caught following Donal yesterday. There's something wrong about him, but I dinna ken what it is. Only that I think Donal is in danger from him. And serving a laird, he has free run of the glen and the Aerie. He has bollocks aplenty to come in here, to be seen and recognized. He's confident—too sure of himself. I dinna like it."

"I saw him frown at ye." Drummond shrugged it off. "'Tis not as though he made a threat. Ye dinna ken what thought crossed his mind while he wore that expression."

"I do. He didna like seeing me there. He kens I could make trouble for him. I smiled back, which is sure to annoy him. Or at least unsettle him."

"Best ye stay aware of where he is and what he's doing. He could be a danger to ye as well," Toran told him.

"I will. Da, does Clan MacThomas have a reason to take issue with Donal? Or MacBean?"

Toran shook his head. "Not that I'm aware. I'll talk to Donal and see if he kens any reason why he'd be of special interest to those lairds, or one of their guards."

"I think 'tis wise," Tavish agreed. "Donal is more than able to take care of himself, but better so if he's watchful. I got the impression last night that, had I not come along, he might have ended the evening with a blade in his back."

"I'll remind Bhaltair to keep an eye on the guard," Drummond said. "Shouldn't we ask his laird to keep him down in the glen and use another man for assistance while he's in the keep?"

Toran shook his head. "Not yet. Let's not make more of this than it is. Not until we find out more, aye? If he's up to something, best we watch and wait. As long as he thinks only ye suspect him, he may still make a move to condemn himself." He smiled grimly as both his sons nodded. "Now, we should get something to eat," he said, his gaze on Tavish. "We've more to discuss with the lairds this afternoon." He gestured for Tavish to precede them from the solar.

Tavish took the hint and left the laird and the heir to discuss whatever Toran intended to convey in private. In the great hall, he quickly located Kilgore sitting at the same table two lairds and other men occupied, but a few seats away from them. Donal was walking toward two women. One was the

MacKyrie laird and Seer, his wife. The other...Tavish paused and tried not to stare. It was her, the lass in his dreams. Had she come with them? Was she the laird's maid? Or was he the father she'd threatened him with?

Tavish walked slowly in their direction and kept his gaze roving, as if searching for someone in the crowded hall. As he approached, Donal was speaking. Tavish passed behind him in time to hear him say, *daughter, ye mustna fash.* The lass was the daughter of the MacKyrie laird and Donal MacNabb? Perhaps his dreams *were* meant to make him aware of a threat to her father rather than a danger to her.

Deep in thought, Tavish found a seat where he could oversee the hall and ate his meal in silence, watching the MacKyrie lass. He noted again that Kilgore seemed very much alone, despite being surrounded by men he'd positioned himself with in the solar. That interested Tavish a great deal. He also watched the other lairds and their men, and the serving lasses. He paid special attention to who talked to whom, and the tenor of the looks shared between the visitors. The only significance to all he observed was the lack of any conversation, even any eye contact, between Kilgore and any of the lairds he stood behind in the solar. If their relationship was so poor, why had any the laird brought this man with him?

When Donal and his family left the hall, Tavish relaxed. Kilgore remained in his seat. Unless the danger extended beyond Kilgore, Donal should be safe. Toran would tell Donal what Tavish had observed and done to keep him safe. Then Donal would be doubly vigilant and Tavish could focus on protecting the man's daughter, as he'd intended.

7

The next morning, Aileana summoned Tavish to her herbal to meet with the MacKyrie Seer. The prospect of being examined by the mother of the woman he saw in his visions made him sweat, but he knew his mother believed the Seer could help him. If anything she did let him see the source of danger to her daughter, he'd cooperate in every way he could.

"I have done for Ellie everything she needs," Aileana told him. "She is well, and she rested well overnight." She gestured him to a seat and settled herself to wait until Ellie MacKyrie arrived. In moments, she walked in looking much better and less tired than she had the evening before. Tavish rose and offered her his seat.

"Thank ye, nay. I want ye to sit and relax," she said and he sank back down. Then she turned to Aileana. "Healer, I'd appreciate if ye would monitor us both, if ye can."

"One at a time?"

"Nay, together, at the same time. Can ye do such as that?"

"I believe so. What can ye tell me about what I may expect to sense?"

"Honestly, I dinna ken. Tavish's talent is unexpected. I have always believed male seers are rare. I never expected to meet one, but it may be simply that others keep their abilities hidden. Tavish, did ye have visions or dreams as a young lad?"

"Nay, Seer. This started after...my voice changed."

"Ah, of course."

"Then, I had only wee glimpses. But it has been happening more often and more clearly ever since. Still, it seems to happen at random, and sometimes a vision comes true, but often does not. 'Tis naught I can summon or control."

"Verra well. I want ye to close yer eyes, take slow, deep breaths. Let yer mind clear of all thoughts. Hear yer breath and my voice."

She must have gestured to his mother because suddenly, he felt her touch on his arm, and a strange doubling of sensation that must be her link to the Seer.

"Breathe, lad," Ellie murmured.

He did as she bade, clearing his mind as though preparing for sleep. Nothing happened for the longest time, then suddenly, he was in the same vision he'd been having for weeks, following along a darkened stone wall, turning a corner, seeing a lass, then losing sight of her. There, as it had before, the vision ended.

He jerked awake, knocking his mother's hand from his arm. Suddenly, light dazzled his eyes, and a headache pounded somewhere in the middle of his head. That was new. "What happened?"

Both his mother and Ellie rubbed their foreheads, as if their pain was centered there.

"What did ye sense, Healer?" The Seer's gaze fixed on his mother.

"I...I'm not certain I ken. At first, ye both seemed to sleep. Then something changed in Tavish, and I think ye got a sense of what he experienced through me?"

Had Ellie seen what he saw? Had she seen her daughter?

"Only a faint echo, I think. I didna see a vision, though I suspect ye did," she said and turned her penetrating gaze to him. "I sensed only an impression of yer familiarity with what ye were seeing. That and dismay. What did ye see, Tavish?"

How much should he tell her? Could he enlist her aid in protecting her daughter? Or would the content of his dreams upset her too much? She'd been ill for a long time and only just recovered. If only he could talk to his mother privately first, perhaps she would know.

But Ellie MacKyrie waited, her gaze boring into him. "Tell me, lad."

He nodded, knowing that telling her was the right decision, even if it upset her. She would want to protect her child, and she could not do that if she remained ignorant. "'Twas the same vision I've been having for weeks. I'm walking somewhere in the keep. 'Tis dark. There is a stone wall beside me. I canna tell if 'tis outside or in a hallway. I have a strong sense of disquiet. Even danger. In the last few weeks, I began to see a lass ahead of me, and I've gotten closer and closer to her each time. She turns and glances back at me. I get only a partial glimpse of her face, then she continues on around a corner. That's all I've ever seen. I dinna ken what it means." It was the truth, if not all he knew.

"Who is the lass? Is she here?"

Tavish should have counted on Aileana's natural curiosity to prompt her to ask questions. He pursed his lips, then sighed and spoke. "She is. I overheard Donal in the great hall call her daughter. She must be yers, too?" Tavish did his best to keep his tone from betraying how deeply the dream had disturbed him.

"Aye, my daughter Yvaine. Ye have been seeing her for weeks? And ye havena yet met?"

"We have. I—I tried to convince her two days ago to let me

escort her around the castle. To keep her safe. Because of my visions, though I didna tell her that. Perhaps I should have, though given what ye said about male seers, I doubt she would have believed me."

The Seer nodded.

"I'm sure she thought I was simply trying to get close to her, a new and attractive lass," Tavish continued. "She refused and went upstairs. I didna ken at the time who she was, and she never told me her name." He liked the sound of it. *Yvaine*.

"Aye, well," Ellie said, and sighed, then turned to Aileana. "With the bonds between our clans, 'tis hard to believe she'd be in danger here. But," Ellie continued with a nod to Tavish, "a young lass is always at risk among strangers. And yer visions worry me greatly."

Tavish appreciated that she took his warning seriously, even if he couldn't tell from her tone or her expression what she was prepared to do about it.

She thought for a moment, then looked to Aileana. "I have nay doubt both yer sons are busy with the gathering, but I would appreciate someone keeping an eye on her." She returned her gaze to him. "Since ye already offered, I would like ye to continue. Discreetly, if ye can. She resents the idea of an escort, and she would notice my men. But if her father learns of any threat to her, he will lock her away until the time comes for us to leave." She turned back to Aileana. "Yvaine would hate that, but we couldna bear any harm to befall her. 'Tis better Tavish continue as he meant to do and keep watch over her."

"He has my permission, of course," Aileana answered. "Tavish, can ye? I ken yer da wants ye to attend at least some of the gathering."

"Aye, he has so far. I'll do the best I can. And the best Yvaine will allow."

"Thank ye, lad. Now, I think the headache ye gave me has

faded. I believe I will go rest a wee before the midday meal. With as much of a bridge between us as yer mother and I were able to build, ye may find your vision more complete should it come again. As yer mother said, something changed. Time will tell if yer link to me has made ye a stronger Seer."

"Thank ye, Ellie," his mother told her, then elbowed him.

"Aye." Tavish added his thanks. But between possibly amplifying his visions and consigning her daughter to his care, he wondered what his mother and the MacKyrie laird and Seer had gotten him into now.

TAVISH FOUND HIS TWIN, EILIDH IN THE NURSERY.

"How did ye ken I was here?" She rose from her chair and came to him. "What has happened? Ye wouldna seek me out unless something had."

"One of the maids saw ye headed this way," he answered, ignoring her second question. "What are ye doing up here?"

"Flora asked me to watch the weans for a few minutes while she got something to eat." She gestured to the children in her temporary charge, ranging in age from six-year-old Rory, Drummond and Morven's son, to several infants in their cribs. Rory was demonstrating perimeter defense to four-year old Cuddy, who delighted in knocking holes in Rory's carefully constructed fortification. The smaller lad picked up carved toy soldiers here and there and tossed them back to Rory, who seemed to have an unending well of patience. He simply replaced his men and continued on with what he was doing.

Tavish nodded toward him. "That's a good lad. His mother is weaving today?"

"Aye. Morven said she needed to get away from the crowd and her work was her best refuge. Ferelith is there, too, at her loom. I canna wait to see what they create." She paused and turned her attention to her brother's face. "Now, tell me why ye are here. Something is amiss," she said with that certainty of each other's moods that they shared. "What is bothering ye, Tavish?"

He crossed his arms. "It turns out the lass in my visions is the daughter of Donal MacNabb and the MacKyrie laird."

Eilidh's eyes widened. "Interesting. She should be well-raised and perhaps even with a talent like her mother's and yers. That shouldna be a problem for ye. So, what has ye *fashed*?"

Eilidh had a gleam in her eye that made Tavish wonder if she knew exactly who Yvaine was, and had for some time. "Am I the only one who didna ken that?"

"Of the two of us, aye. I met her the day before yesterday."

"And why didna ye tell me?"

"When have we even seen each other since then, must less had a chance to speak?"

"Aye, well, mayhap ye are right. We've both been pulled in different directions for the last two days."

"So, answer my question, brother dear."

"Besides the fact that she could be in danger? I tried to tell her that the first time I saw her, before we were even introduced —which we still have not been. I offered to escort her. To protect her. She refused, of course. She thinks me at best an annoyance. At worst? I dinna ken. But here's the problem. Her mother wants me to stay close to her. I dinna ken how I can, since Yvaine apparently hates me."

"Tell her ye are acting at her mother and laird's request. Surely, she canna refuse ye after that?"

"I'm not so certain. She seems strong-willed enough to refuse, no matter her mother's wishes."

"What about her da?"

"Donal MacNabb?"

"Surely he'll want her to remain safe."

"Aye, but he can simply confine her to her chamber, something I got the sense her mother wouldna approve, but might accept."

Eilidh patted his shoulder. "I ken ye well, brother. Ye will find a way to win over Yvaine. There is not a lass alive who can resist ye when ye set your mind to it."

Tavish laughed. "If only that were true."

"Have faith, brother. She's in yer visions for a reason. Ye just dinna ken what that reason is. Yet."

AFTER THE MIDDAY MEAL, YVAINE'S FATHER WENT BACK TO THE Lathan laird's solar and her mother went to meet with his wife, the healer. That left her at loose ends, but she was certain of one thing. She needed some time out of her chamber. She settled by the hearth for a few minutes, watching people come and go and wondering if Tavish Lathan would try to join her. He'd disappeared from the meal before her parents went their separate ways.

His sister had spoken highly of him, but Yvaine trusted her own impressions more. Was she actually sitting here, waiting for him? She chided herself for letting her curiosity get the better of her common sense. She needed to do something useful, then decided to check on the puppies, before visiting the weavers to watch their work and learn what she could.

A man went down the short hall to the laird's solar, and soon after, the big guard Eilidh had described to her left it and spoke quietly to a pair of men sitting near the keep's door, then they all went outside. That was interesting. She stood, but before she could leave, men poured out of the laird's solar and headed outside.

She followed them.

Her father was among them. They were talking as they went, and she did not like what she heard. They'd been called out of the keep to deal with fights in the tent encampment down in the glen. She waited in the bailey while he and the others disappeared into the stables.

A little while later, they reappeared on horseback and rode out of the Aerie's gates.

She took some comfort in the fact that a man she recognized from Eilidh's description—the big Lathan head guard, Bhaltair—and a dozen more men accompanied her father. Still, Yvaine was not happy to see Donal riding into trouble. But knowing him, he'd volunteered to help quell the disturbance.

There was nothing she could do save stand in the gate and watch them ride down the tor. The guards had strict instructions to keep all the lasses in the Aerie, so they wouldn't let her follow. Not that she would. She was Donal MacNabb's daughter, savvy enough to know that her presence would distract him and put him in even more danger.

She'd been there only a few minutes when her persistent shadow, Tavish, walked up beside her. "He'll be alright," he told her, as if he could read her mind. "According to my da, Donal is one of the most wily and accomplished warriors in Scotland. Dinna let his age fool ye. He can still take care of himself."

"And ye would ken this, how?" She rounded on him. Tavish Lathan always seemed to make himself the perfect target of her frustrations about everything that perplexed and aggravated her on this trip. Her stomach clenched along with her fists.

He noticed her hands and smiled. "From talking to my da and yer mother."

"When did ye talk to my mother? Why?"

He shrugged and dropped his gaze to his boots. "'Tis a small matter of my talent. My mother thought yers could help me. Perhaps she did. 'Tis too soon to tell."

"How could my mother help...?" She went silent for a moment, then her eyes widened. "Ye are a Seer?"

"Not much of one, at least not yet, but aye."

Yvaine didn't think much could shock her, but that admission did. A Lathan lad, son of the much-respected healer, was a Seer? "How is that possible? Yer mother is a healer."

"And two sisters and a brother are also healers. My eldest brother can find things—and people. Lately, he has demonstrated he has a little of the healing talent, as well. I'm the odd one, though I've learned I have a touch of the healing talent, too."

He said it with such resignation that she found herself feeling sorry for him. "These abilities have come on ye recently?"

"Aye. Mostly the visions. Dimly. At first, I thought I was merely recalling dreams. Until one of them came true right before my eyes the morning after I saw it. A lass fell from her horse and broke her arm just as I'd seen it the night before."

"I'm sorry for the lass."

"I was, too. But many—most, in truth—do not come true. The next night, I dreamed one of Cook's helpers spilled a kettle of stew. That never happened, though another knocked over a pitcher of milk the next day. Yer mother thinks my visions will become more accurate over time. Until then, I dinna ken which to believe, which to trust, and which to ignore."

Yvaine could sympathize. Her talent behaved much the same way, and her mother had told her exactly the same. That it would strengthen and grow more reliable over time. Should she tell Tavish?

"There's one dream I've had often, and it involves ye," Tavish said reluctantly, softly, as if he fought a battle within himself to share this information.

"About me?" She backed up a pace. If his dreams involved

some attraction to her, no wonder he'd sought her out. But what would he do about them? Heat lanced through Yvaine. "Tell me what ye've seen."

"'Tis not like that." He held up both hands, as if recognizing and denying her leap to a conclusion she didn't like. "Even before I met ye, I saw ye walking along a stone wall. Somewhere nearby. I canna tell if 'tis inside the keep or somewhere outside. 'Tis fairly dark. Ye look back at me for a moment, then continue on until ye turn a corner. Then I usually wake up." He opened his mouth as if to continue speaking, then pressed his lips together and closed his eyes as if trying to picture the scene before opening them again and meeting her gaze.

She fought not to stare at his lips. They looked firm and despite her antipathy for him, she wondered how they would feel on her lips, or on the shell of her ear, or whispering along her throat. A tingle ran down the side of her neck to the juncture with her shoulder. She shook it off. "What does it mean?"

"I dinna ken, but I have a strong sense of foreboding. Of danger."

Her heart beat faster in her chest. "What kind of danger?"

"I dinna ken. 'Tis why I offered to escort ye. To keep ye safe. To protect ye from whatever it is—or might be."

She couldn't believe she was in any danger. Why would she be? But perhaps Tavish's visions were somehow related to her premonitions about her father. Could she accept that all this time, he'd truly been trying to protect her? And should she tell him, or would that admission make him even more determined to remain by her side? "Ye said ye usually wake up when I turn the corner. What happens when ye remain asleep?"

He colored and looked away. "I—I canna tell ye. Not yet. So far, I simply wake up."

"Are ye certain ye havena seen more?"

"Nay." He pursed his lips and stared down the tor at the tent encampment. Yvaine's gaze followed his, recalling her to why they were standing here. There was no sign of the riders, no sign of violence underway. It looked peaceful. But the appearance of peace might be deceptive. She hoped her father and the Lathans had gotten whatever summoned them to the glen under control.

8

If only he held his bow and quiver, Kilgore thought as he watched more than a dozen men ride through the Aerie's gates and start down the tor. The man he longed to kill rode right toward him. With one well-placed arrow, he could take his revenge and then slip into the trees behind the tent encampment, and no one would ever ken who had taken out the great Donal MacNabb. The man who killed his laird. The man who made his clan subject to MacKyrie, whose chief was a lass. He shook his head, aggrieved at the idea.

Instead, he'd have to chance throwing his blade, or if MacNabb made the mistake of dismounting, getting close enough in a crowd to plunge a knife in his back without anyone seeing who'd done the deed. And if he was successful, but caught? He'd come here willing to give his life to avenge his grandfather and the loss of his clan's autonomy. If that was the only way, then so be it. But he preferred to live, and to enjoy his victory.

So far, his plan had worked. The fight he'd started had drawn down Lathan guards. He intended to keep the camp in the glen stirred up, the Lathan guards busy here—as many as he could attract from their duty guarding the Aerie—while he roamed the keep at will and found his quarry, alone. He'd nearly succeeded, except for the interference of that Lathan. Tavish. He'd been in the laird's solar, too, and seen him again. Going in there might have been a mistake. He'd been seen twice. He was known. He needed to act fast and escape before he attracted any more attention to himself.

As the guards approached, he kept his hands visible and his gaze down, save for glances sufficient to see where MacNabb went. Several of the guards split away from the rest and rode through the camp. But a core of six remained together around the man he wanted. Bollocks. He needed a distraction.

"Damned Lathans," he muttered just loudly enough for those nearby to hear, but not the approaching mounted men. "Who do they think they are? This is our camp."

"Aye," another man nearby said. "Our camp. We dinna need Lathan guards in our midst."

The next volley came louder and from several sources. Men, Kilgore suspected, who'd spent the day drinking, bored, and spoiling for a fight.

The mounted contingent kept coming, led by one of the largest warriors Kilgore had ever seen. That didn't worry him. The bigger they were, the slower, in his experience. He could gut the man and dance out of the way of his fall before he had a chance to react. But he wouldn't waste his effort there. MacNabb rode half a length behind and to the side of the bigger man.

Someone yelled threats. Someone, perhaps the same person, threw a cup, barely missing the big man in the lead, who saw it coming and leaned aside. He didn't bother to pull a blade. He simply favored the man with a cold stare and rode past him.

That seemed to settle down the unrest Kilgore had started. Frustrated, he gritted his teeth and slipped behind a few other men, making certain he had an escape route between tents directly behind him. Then he waited and watched until MacNabb drew within range. His and the other guards' gazes raked the crowd, never ceasing to move, to study faces. Then someone on the other side of the riders shouted another obscenity, drawing their attention away.

Kilgore took advantage of the diversion and threw his dirk. As it flew, one of the guards' horses shied and MacNabb turned to see what caused the commotion. Instead of burying itself in his chest, the blade lodged in the meat of his upper arm. The warriors around him reacted immediately, closing ranks.

The group around Kilgore stirred and backed up as MacNabb pulled the blade free, stared at it for a moment, then dropped it in the dirt. Kilgore swore, certain that he'd never recover the blade his father had passed down to him, and worse, he had failed to kill his target. MacNabb knew what it looked like. Being seen carrying it would betray him.

He left it behind and moved with the crowd, making certain to relieve one of them of his dirk and slipping it into his own sheath. Then he faded between the tents on his escape route, moved behind them, and kept going. So did most of the men near him. He depended on the confusion to help him blend in.

He didn't get far. Men on horseback converged and rounded up anyone nearby. Someone must have taken MacNabb up the tor. In the confusion, he hadn't seen, but the guards would not be free to hunt the attacker unless they hastened him away. Kilgore fingered the hilt of the dirk in his sheath. It wouldn't do to be caught without one. Or with one that matched the blade he'd thrown. This one didn't. And he could point to it and proclaim his innocence. So could every other man there, save the man whose dirk this was. Would they kill him? Kilgore didn't care. Taking down MacNabb was worth a life. He only regretted that his blow had missed killing his target.

Yvaine grabbed Tavish's arm and pointed when she saw the riders appear in the camp, moving swiftly as if searching for something. Or someone? Raised voices reached them on the top of the tor. There must be a fight underway. She couldn't see it, but Tavish nodded.

"Something is happening," he said.

His frown told her he was as worried as she. "I canna just stand here while Da is down there."

"Ye can and ye will," Tavish said, his gaze still on the glen, but his voice stern. "That camp is nay place for a lass, and if there's a fight underway, 'tis even more dangerous to ye. We must stay here and let Bhaltair and his men handle it."

She knew he was right. Her comment had been a foolish thing to say. But if she was a lad, she'd be fighting at her father's side, not standing here, waiting with Tavish Lathan. She'd worried about her da for so long, staying here was almost more than she could take.

Before long, riders began to mount the trail up the tor. Yvaine waited, fairly bouncing on her toes, to see that her father was with them and unharmed.

She gasped when she spotted him. "Da!" His left sleeve was torn and red with blood. His arm hung at his side. Pulling free of the hand Tavish placed on her shoulder, she ran past the gate guard and down the tor to meet him. Tavish chased her down and pulled her out of the way of the horses, against the inside wall of the path.

"Ye daft lass! Do ye want to get killed? There's barely enough room for the horses."

He was angry. She could hear it in his voice, but her attention riveted to her father.

As soon as he got close, she called to him again. "Da!"

He looked up at her cry and frowned. "Yvaine, what are ye

doing out here? Get back inside the gate. Tavish, get her moving."

"Da, ye are hurt!"

"No worse than I have been before." One-handed, he reined up beside them, stopping the men behind him as well. "Lad, get her back inside the gates, or I'll have yer head on a pike. Carry her if she'll not move on her own two feet."

"Nay! I'll stay with ye, Da."

Donal gave Tavish a fierce stare.

"As ye wish," Tavish said.

Before she realized his intent, he picked her up, then tossed her over his shoulder, turned and started up the path.

She kicked and cursed him, but he kept a tight grip on her. Laughter from the men on the walls above them and from the horsemen arrayed below them echoed and added to her fury. "Put me down, damn ye! Who do ye think ye are?" With closed fists, she hit him everywhere she could reach. Lucky for him, she couldn't touch bare skin, or she'd claw him down to the muscle.

"I'm just doing what yer da asked me to do," Tavish said mildly. "We'll be inside the gates in a minute, and then ye can see to him. I'm fond of my head right where it is. I'd rather listen to ye screech than disobey yer da."

"Screech!" She choked and panted. It wasn't easy to breathe with his shoulder in her belly. "I dinna have the breath to screech," she complained and pounded on his back again. "But when ye put me down, ye'd best cover yer ears."

Tavish chuckled at that.

Yvaine's fury and mortification spiked. "Ye think this is funny?"

"Nay, lass. I think this is hard work carrying ye up this hill." He grunted when she fisted him in the kidneys. "Ah, here we are. Inside the gates and out of the way of yer da and the rest of the riders."

With that, he bent forward and to the side to let her slide to the ground. She fought him even then and landed hard, groaned, then surged to her feet. He stood over her, smiling.

Smiling!

She slapped him as hard as she could. Then for good measure, did it a second time. "If ye ever touch me again, ye willna have to worry about my da. I'll kill ye myself."

She didn't wait for his reaction. She ran to her father, who was dismounting with some help from the big guard. "Ye need the healer, Da. Who did this?"

"'Twas an accident, lass. I'll be fine."

"Ye are still bleeding. Come, let's find the healer."

"I'm here." Aileana's soothing voice and stately presence calmed some of Yvaine's fear and fury. "A guard fetched me," she told Yvaine with a tight smile. Then she turned to Donal and frowned at his arm. "Donal, who have ye angered now?"

"No one. 'Twas an accident, Aileana. Barely a scratch."

She took his good arm and led him toward the door to the keep.

Yvaine ran after them. "I'm coming with ye."

"Nay, lass," Donal said. "Go tell yer mother where I am. I'll be as good as new very soon."

"Da..."

"Go on, Yvaine. I dinna want Ellie to hear about this from someone else,"

Yvaine followed them into the great hall and watched them go, then did as he told her and headed for the stairs while they turned toward the hallway that led to the herbal. As she climbed the stairs, she recalled every moment since spotting her da coming up the tor. Tavish Lathan had picked her up like a sack of oats! How dare he manhandle the daughter of a laird?

And he hadn't seemed surprised to see her father wounded. Had he seen that this would happen? The first thing he'd said to her as he joined her was "He'll be alright." He must have seen her father injured and the aftermath. Why hadn't Tavish stopped her da from going with the other guards? Because he arrived too late? Or just late enough? The thought made cold chills pebble her skin. The Lathans couldn't be involved. If her father was in danger from his oldest friends, from people he considered family, the situation was even more dire than she'd feared. And she'd just let him walk away with Aileana.

She paused, intending to turn and go back down the stairs. She glanced across the hall, looking for them, and noticed Tavish standing in the middle of the hall, fists on hips, watching her. She gave him a glare, then turned her back and left him standing there. She'd do as her father requested and tell her mother first. But then, she'd join her father in the herbal and do what she could to keep him safe. He might trust the Lathans, but suddenly, she did not.

TAVISH WATCHED YVAINE MOUNT THE STAIRS. LIKE IN HIS VISIONS, her hips swung from side to side with each tread she climbed. Her braid swung in time to her steps, too. His hands clenched and unclenched, the feel of her under them still wildly present in his senses. Her scent. Her outrage. Her slim waist, lush hips and nicely rounded bottom. He wanted all of them under his hands again.

Not bloody likely. She'd threatened to kill him if he ever touched her again. He could thank her father for that. Pick her up, he'd said. Carry her if she willna go under her own power. Tavish hadn't needed to be asked twice. The chance to hold her, in any fashion, was too tempting to refuse. Feeling her hands pounding on his own arse had been worth the burden of carrying her up the tor.

Still, in hindsight, he'd rather not have embarrassed her that way. The laughter that greeted them as they entered the

Aerie's gates must still be ringing in her ears. It was in his. He'd much rather have touched her as a lover might. Or at least as a friend, hand to hand, comfortable with each other and able to share secrets and solve problems together.

He could wish all he wanted. After today, he'd lost any chance of getting close to the lass. He shook his head and turned away as she disappeared around the corner into the hallway at the top of the stairs.

Eilidh would have his head. He never should have picked up Yvaine. He should have taken her arm and dragged her up the hill if necessary, but left her the dignity of remaining on her own two feet.

Why couldn't he do anything right where she was concerned? Was it because he feared for her? Or because he wanted her? That thought stopped him in his tracks.

Shaken, he headed for the one place he knew she would not be expected to go. The laird's solar. He could listen to the deliberations while he gave himself a chance to think. He didn't know her well enough for her to be this important to him. Yet, somehow, she was.

9

After advising her mother that her father was being treated by the Lathan healer for his wound, Yvaine hurried back down to the herbal where Aileana was patching up Donal.

"Leave it," she heard him growl while she was still in the hallway outside. "'Twill heal on its own soon enough. Ye dinna need to suffer it anymore."

His gruff tone told Yvaine the healer had tested his patience since she'd left them. She paused in the doorway and took in the scene. Aileana had removed the sleeve from Donal's left arm. She had done something to stop the bleeding, and was washing away the blood that had run down to his hand.

"And when it festers, ye'll be too far away for me to help ye. And even if ye are not, that is something I'd rather not go through. So, I'll thank ye to *haud yer wheesht* and let me finish tending to yer arm. I'm near to done."

Donal made a noise deep in his throat, but relented and looked away.

Yvaine watched, fascinated, as the healer set aside the bloody cloth, put her hands on either side of the gaping wound, and closed her eyes. That was no scratch. He'd been stabbed. Her stomach sank, and she put a hand over her mouth to stifle a cry. Her forebodings had been true Seeings. He had been in danger. Was he still? Had he killed the person who'd done this? Or were the rest of the guards hunting for the man? She pivoted out of the doorway and leaned her back against the hallway wall, trying to breathe. She needed to calm herself. Try to see if the danger persisted. But nothing came to her.

She took another breath and leaned forward to step into the room. This time, Donal must have seen the motion from the corner of his eye. He turned his gaze to her and shook his head. He didn't want her to enter. She gave him a reluctant nod and held her place until the healer opened her eyes and stepped back.

Even from her position by the door, Yvaine could see the wound had closed. A new, pink scar decorated his arm where the gap had been.

"Verra well, Donal. 'Tis done. Ye are not to use this arm for the rest of the day. In fact, get ye upstairs and lie down."

"I canna do that. I must join yer husband in his solar."

The healer studied him while she rubbed her arm, then sighed. "Promise me ye willna do anything foolish in there. I dinna wish to have to patch ye up again."

His gaze shifted to her arm and he colored. "I promise. I dinna wish to cause ye any more pain."

"Donal!" Ellie pushed past Yvaine and entered the herbal. "How is he, Aileana?"

"Good enough to sit quietly the rest of the day. No fighting. No brawling. If he willna cooperate, take him upstairs and call for me. I'll put a healing sleep on him that will keep him quiet for the next full day."

Yvaine didn't miss the frown he sent the healer's way at that comment.

Her mother took his hand, pulling his attention to her. "Ye understand her, aye? If ye hurt yerself again, ye hurt her, too."

"I ken fine how her talent works," he answered, his tone close to an aggravated snarl. Then his expression softened. "Sorry. I'll behave." He stood and looked ready to leave.

"I need to speak to ye, Da," Yvaine said, stepping into the chamber from where she'd waited in the doorway.

"Let's get ye some food," Ellie told Aileana. "Then ye can rest."

Aileana nodded and left with her, leaving Yvaine to face her father.

"What is it, lass?" He resumed his seat and gestured her to the stool next to his.

Yvaine hesitated. He looked tired. And more subdued, now that the healer and her mother had gone. But he needed to hear her. Yvaine told her father what she'd observed as he and the Lathan guards rode back up the tor. How Tavish didn't seem surprised. "Ye ken I've been fashed about ye, about a threat to ye." She pointed to his arm. "And today ye were stabbed. Did ye catch the man who did it?"

Donal shook his head, his lips flattened into a thin line as he stood.

"With all those guards around ye?" She held up a hand in a mute appeal for him to listen to her, to let her speak. "What if the Lathans are not the friends—the family—ye think they are?"

"Yvaine—"

"What if Tavish holds a grudge over his brother Jamie and the way he left MacKyrie? I've been looking for some stranger to cause problems, but what if the danger is closer to home?"

"Dinna be daft, daughter. I'm in nay danger from any Lathan, even Jamie. We came to an understanding before he left us." He shook his head. "Nay. Ye needna fash about them. Now that this has happened," he said, lifted his newly healed left arm and grimaced, "perhaps this is what ye sensed would happen. He took her hand with his right hand. "I'm well and will remain so. Now, go find yer mother and the healer and join them. I'm going to find a clean shirt, then go to Toran's solar for a wee."

"Da, ye must listen to me."

"Have ye seen any other threat?"

"Nay, but…"

"Nay," he barked, then sighed. "There isna another. Ye are upset, 'tis all." He settled back onto the stool and crossed his arms. Muscle bulged, stretching the newly healed scar, and he winced.

That small change of expression in her normally stoic father told her he was more shaken up than he wanted her to see, and that realization shook her. Her father, her hero, was not as invincible as she'd imagined him to be when she was a wee lass. Nay, her dreams, her sense of foreboding gave the lie to that. "Promise me ye will be careful. I dinna think this is over."

"I'm always careful, daughter."

He stood and walked out, leaving her sitting in the herbal, watching his back as he moved away from her. His newly healed arm swung at his side, moving as easily, as firmly, as the other one. As if nothing had ever happened to it. She wrapped her arms around herself as he disappeared, worried that knowing Aileana was here to heal him made him reckless.

Then she groaned. She'd been so worried about him that she hadn't even berated him for telling Tavish to pick her up and carry her up the tor. She'd save that conversation for later, when her father looked more himself. He'd embarrassed her. Perhaps he'd been half out of his head with lost blood or still stirred up from the fight. Either way, it had been a cruel jest, and she would have his apology. Later, when he felt better.

Perhaps by then, he'd realize what he'd done and offer it without her prompting.

YVAINE HEADED OUT INTO THE GREAT HALL, BUT PAUSED AT THE entry, looking for Tavish. She didn't want to see him or speak to him, so she was perfectly happy to find him missing. None of the men sitting at tables had gone down to the glen—and back up—with her father. No one looked at her. No one laughed.

Relieved, she ventured out. Then she spotted her mother and the healer at a table facing the hearth. She crossed the hall, moving around trestle tables and dodging serving lasses, some scrubbing empty tables and some laden with the last remains of the midday meal.

Before she could reach them, she heard the healer laugh. "That's an interesting idea, Ellie," she said. "If we wed Tavish and Yvaine together, think how strong their children's talents could be. Especially if they were seers."

"I think 'tis possible. What an intriguing notion!"

Yvaine stopped, shocked. Marry her and Tavish together? Was her mother out of her mind? Did she know how he'd embarrassed her just hours ago? Nay, she would never marry Tavish Lathan, no matter how her mother and the healer schemed.

She turned away, not willing to be drawn into such a discussion. But where could she go? She was tired of her chamber, and didn't dare go out into the bailey where she might encounter more of the Lathan guards who'd seen her humiliation.

Finally, she chose a seat as far from the healer and her mother as she could find on the other side of the hall, and requested food. After the day's events, she should have no appetite, but suddenly she was ravenous.

A man she didn't know approached her. "Is this seat taken?" He pointed to the one across from her.

She didn't recognize him, so she didn't think he'd seen her humiliation at Tavish's hands. Nothing about this man was particularly memorable. And she had been upside down over Tavish's shoulder. She could have easily missed seeing him. But there was no glint of malicious humor in his eye. He wasn't laughing at her. He simply asked for a place to sit and eat. She glanced around. It was midafternoon, and there were plenty of empty places. Why would he choose to sit across from her? Still, she couldn't think of a reason to deny this man the seat. If she became uncomfortable, she could join the healer and her mother on the other side of the hall. She inclined her head. "Nay, 'tis free."

He sat down with a sigh. "Thank ye. I was hoping for some amiable company. But 'twill be a relief to head home in a few days," he said while he waited for a trencher to be placed before him. "The food here is good. Thank ye," he said and smiled up at the serving lass who brought his meal, meeting her gaze with his own. She dipped a shallow curtsy, smiled, and went on her way with a little added sway to her walk.

Ah, he was a charmer then, this one, using cleverly timed polite words to accomplish what, for men as attractive as Tavish, could be done with looks and a small flex of muscle alone. She wished Tavish had a bit more of this man's polite charm and less of the Lathan good looks. It might improve his attractiveness to her overall.

"But I'd rather sleep in my cot in the barracks than on the ground in a tent," he added and turned his attention to his meal.

Despite her misgivings about him, curiosity got the better of her. "Ye dinna have a wife, or a lass waiting for ye at home?"

"Nay. No one." He took a drink and shrugged. "Someday, perhaps."

He dug in, so Yvaine did the same, watching him under lowered lashes. His table manners were good, and he was modestly attractive, with dark hair and strong shoulders, though they were not as broad as Tavish's. A thin scar ran from his jaw across his cheek toward his ear. It looked more like a training wound that a battle wound, but she couldn't really judge, save that it was thin and faint. Long healed, then. Perhaps even a wound from childhood.

"What about ye, lass? Is there a lad at home, pining for ye?"

She chuckled at that. "Nay, not that I ken."

"How can that be, for a beautiful lass such as ye?"

"Dinna flatter me, sir. I dinna need it."

"Verra well. Perhaps ye will tell me yer name?"

"Yvaine. And yers?"

The man smiled and answered, "Iver."

"Pleased to meet ye," she remarked. She didn't really ken if she was, but it never hurt to be pleasant.

"So, ye are not a Lathan?"

She saw no harm in telling him. "Nay, MacKyrie."

He colored and for a moment, she thought he'd choked on a bite of food. Finally, he swallowed and nodded. "Good clan."

That seemed to end the conversation. She kept her gaze lowered but continued to watch him through her lashes. He consumed his meal, all the while lifting his gaze to study her. Did her name hold some significance to him that he hadn't shared with her? Or was he just showing interest in a new lass as her father had warned would happen?

He finished his meal before she did and stood.

"'Twas good to meet ye, Yvaine MacKyrie. I hope we'll meet again before 'tis time for all of us to leave here."

"I, too," she said, and found she meant it. It would be good to have an ally other than the Lathans for the time she remained here. And seeing her with another man might divert her mother and the healer's scheme for her and Tavish Lathan.

Aye, her new friend might be just what she needed to spoil their plans.

Donal chose that moment to walk up and greet her.

"Good day to ye, sir," Iver said. "I was just leaving."

But then she noticed he hadn't quite finished his meal. Was he being polite, leaving the seat to her father? Or was he eager to get away from him? He had the oddest expression on his face, narrow-eyed and flushed, but only for a moment. Then he took a breath, looked away from her father and left them alone.

Donal watched him walk away for a moment, then said, "Daughter. What are ye doing over here? Why are ye not sitting with yer mother?"

"I didna wish to disturb her and the healer. They seemed to be having a serious discussion." Serious indeed, planning her future with Tavish Lathan. She hid her dismay and kept her expression placid.

"I was going to go back to the gathering, but I dinna want to leave ye here, alone. Ye should join them."

He didn't say it, but she could tell he wasn't happy that she'd been sitting with a stranger. At least he had put on a clean shirt and looked better than when he left her in the healer's herbal. Given the time since she'd last seen him, he must have taken a few minutes to rest and refresh himself.

"I was actually going to visit the weavers as soon as I finished eating," she told him, then froze. Tavish Lathan was coming their way.

TAVISH SPOTTED YVAINE AND DONAL AT A NEARBY TABLE. HE also noticed Kilgore, the man he suspected of stalking Donal, walking away from him and Yvaine. He put down his nearly empty trencher for a serving lass to clear away, then he left the hall.

He'd been eating with Donal and Yvaine? Perhaps Tavish had been wrong to suspect him. Perhaps they'd been acquainted all along. Surely by now, his father would have had a chance to tell Donal that Tavish had stopped that man from following him. Perhaps Toran hadn't mentioned it again to Tavish because Donal assured him he knew the man.

Tavish went to where Donal stood by his daughter. "Good day, Donal, Yvaine," he greeted them.

"Tavish, sit with us," Donal invited.

Tavish was only too glad to take him up on the offer. His daughter, it appeared, was less enthusiastic.

She frowned at her father, then turned a glare on him. "Please, do," she said evenly, though her expression was anything but welcoming.

He sat. "Who was the man ye were just speaking with?" He kept his tone mild, though curiosity burned within him to find out what connection they had to him.

"A friend of my daughter's," Donal replied, giving her a frown.

"Did ye meet him here or do ye ken him from somewhere else?"

"Here," she answered shortly. Her frown intensified. "Why do ye ask?"

He would not upset her by telling her he'd stopped the man from following her father. He'd save that news for Donal when he had a chance to tell him alone, since it appeared his own father hadn't, or if he had, Donal had discounted the threat. Had the MacKyrie Seer said anything to Donal yet about Tavish's visions? Donal didn't seem perturbed, so perhaps she hadn't yet had the chance.

"Just curious," he told her.

If Tavish had stopped this Kilgore from whatever he meant to do with Donal, the man might now have turned his attention to McNabb's daughter as a way to get to him. Donal needed to know that. Then he could deal with Yvaine, who would likely have told Tavish to mind his own business. She'd say it was none of his affair whom she made friends with, but she'd be wrong.

A serving lass brought a trencher of bread and cheese. Donal began eating and seemed to pay no attention to the few people around them. Then again, Donal was such an accomplished warrior that it might only seemed like he was paying no attention.

Had his wife told him she had asked Tavish to keep an eye on their daughter? Did he approve and was leaving Tavish to do whatever he could to get back in Yvaine's good graces? Tavish could think of only one way to begin that process. "Yvaine, I owe ye an apology." From the corner of his eye, he saw Donal pause his chewing, then resume again. "I shouldna have embarrassed ye on the path up the tor as I did."

"Nay, ye shouldna," she allowed. But she glanced at her father, making Tavish's spirits lift, just a little.

"Ye should ken, I'm sorry for it."

Her words were clipped when she told him, "Ye are not the only one who owes me an apology."

Her flat statement startled Tavish. So did the glare she shot her father.

"Dinna look at me," Donal said. "Ye got what ye deserved."

"What!" Yvaine's outrage was clear, even though she kept her voice down and stayed in her seat.

"Ye should never have run down the tor into the midst of the horses. Ye couldha been killed," Donal answered, lifting his gaze to her. "Tavish did only as I asked to keep ye safe."

Tavish didn't recall any asking being involved. More like a direct order and a threat to separate his head from his body. But suddenly, he had even more sympathy for Yvaine than he'd had from worrying for her in his visions. Aye, she'd put herself in danger, but her father's response had not needed to be so harsh. Still, he'd been wounded, and seeing his daughter put herself at risk must have frightened and infuriated him.

"In truth, daughter, ye owe Tavish an apology. Ye put him at risk as well."

Donal's words could not have shocked Tavish more if he'd ordered them to wed on the spot.

"Ye expect me to apologize to the man who carried me over his shoulder and made me a laughingstock?"

"Ye are alive and unharmed, are ye not? And I dinna hear anyone laughing now. 'Twas but a moment's relief after the—incident—in the glen." He lifted his formerly wounded arm, then turned to Tavish. "Ye ken how after a fight, men need to let off steam. To laugh."

"Of course," Tavish said, though he could think of other things men liked to do after a battle, but he'd not mention them in front of this man's daughter, certainly not with Donal sitting right there. "I'm sure they didna mean anything by it."

"Well, good for ye," Yvaine spat. "Ye are not the one they were laughing at."

"Were they not?" Donal asked her. "Who obeyed me and carried ye? Think ye Tavish didna regret the eyes on him every step up that hill with ye over his shoulder, spitting and snarling and pounding on his arse?"

Tavish nodded, but in truth, he hadn't thought of it that way. He'd assumed the laughter was all for Yvaine's position over his shoulder, and her reaction to it. Still, now that he mentioned it, he could see Donal's point. He must have looked equally ridiculous.

Yvaine's gaze remained down. She sat quietly for a long moment, then said, "Very well, I'm sorry, too," so softly, Tavish might have missed it had he not been looking at her. She said it reluctantly, he was sure, but she got the words out, no matter how it pained her.

"Thank ye," he told her, then shifted his gaze to her da. "But let me be clear. I will never do anything like that to her again, sir. 'Twas not my intention to see her harmed in any way. *Any* way," he added for emphasis, making it clear he meant more than physical harm. "She deserves to retain her dignity as much as do I, or ye." Before Donal could reply, Tavish continued. "Aye, she was in danger, as was I for chasing her down the tor, but the horses would naturally avoid us, and the trail was— barely—wide enough for them to do so. Ye were wounded and perhaps, fraught with the discomfort and the residue of the battle. Even if ye couldna, I should have thought before I acted. I could have avoided the harm I did her."

He glanced aside at Yvaine. She was watching him, flushed and open-mouthed. At his confession? Or at his defiance of her father? Either way, she seemed to regard him with new-found respect. If she did, he was satisfied.

Donal cleared his throat. "Well said, Tavish. But recall this. No matter how wounded, no matter how fraught, as ye say, I might be from a battle, I expect my orders to be followed without question."

"Then 'tis good I dinna fight for yer clan," Tavish said, and stood. "I begin to see why Jamie left MacKyrie," he added, turned, and walked from the table, half expecting Donal's blade to lodge in his back. Instead, he heard the man laugh, and heard Yvaine say, "Da! Stop it. That was poorly done."

Fighting a grin at her defense of him, he left the great hall in a better mood than he had enjoyed in days. His apology had accomplished what he'd hoped and smoothed things over with Yvaine. Her father's refusal to do the same had made Tavish look even better in comparison.

10

Kilgore had left the great hall with his meal a roiling lump in his belly, excitement filling him. He headed down the tor on his way back to his tent in the glen.

Yvaine MacKyrie? She was indeed Donal MacNabb's daughter. He wouldn't have believed it if the man he'd stabbed just hours before hadn't walked up and made their relationship clear.

And why was MacNabb walking about already? He was certain his dirk had penetrated the man's upper arm. Aye, he'd seen it there and he'd seen MacNabb pull it out. Shouldn't he at least have that arm in a sling? It made no sense. Damn the luck for MacNabb to turn away just as he threw. That dirk should have lodged in his chest and killed him.

By now, it was safe to return to the glen. He'd gotten away cleanly. No one had seen him throw the dirk. And no one would be able to identify him. He'd disappeared too quickly into the crowd, lifted without anyone's notice the dirk he now carried, and gotten away.

He heard they'd detained the man who's dirk he now wore —the only man in the crowd without one. But his friends had sworn he was not the attacker. They'd been all around him at the time, cups of ale in hand. He could not have done what the Lathan guards accused. Which meant they were still looking for the man who threw the blade. If anyone had seen him do it —but nay, so far he was still a free man.

Since yesterday, he'd been in and out of the Aerie's gate several times without difficulty. Just another visiting guardsman like all the others coming and going at their lairds' behest, no one special. He would continue to come and go several times a day, letting the guards see him and discount his presence as routine.

He'd even spoken to his intended victim just minutes ago. No light of recognition had dawned in MacNabb's gaze. No guards had gathered around to detain him. He could still achieve his goal.

Then again...he'd missed killing the man earlier today. MacNabb would be more alert to any threat, as would the men around him. He would be harder to get to, more prepared for an attack.

But perhaps his revenge was best taken in a way that would keep the man alive and in pain. By killing his lovely daughter instead. The idea had merit. She'd be easier to manipulate. Easier to get alone. He could even have his way with her before he killed her. She would fight him. He would enjoy subduing her, making her beg, watching her plead for her purity, then, when she realized he meant to kill her, for her life.

The lass had played right into his hands. He'd taken advantage of her upbringing. Most lasses were raised to be polite, if wary, to strangers. Pure chance had led him to that seat and given him the opportunity to get her name. Once he'd achieved what he came here to do, he'd make sure the MacKyrie laird knew about the connection between Kilgore and Clan MacDuff. He wanted her to know who took revenge on her husband. Or on her daughter. Even better, on both. How was it that no one here knew? Kilgore was a powerful family within Clan MacDuff. He enjoyed living dangerously, and using the name Kilgore should have tipped someone to wonder about him. But, it hadn't. Only that Lathan who'd stopped him from following MacNabb suspected him, and he doubted the Lathan knew.

He'd taken another chance today, continuing to sit with her once he knew her name, being charming until he'd seen her father approaching, letting her think him someone she could trust. It was going well until her father arrived. He'd left.

He'd often been told he resembled his grandda. Would MacNabb recognize him? If he saw him and heard the name Kilgore, would he figure it out? So far, he hadn't, and by now, that Lathan whelp must have told someone about detaining him the other night.

Kilgore considered the daughter. He'd created enough of a basis to continue to speak to her. If he could get her alone, he would have his revenge. Perhaps it would not be as satisfying as killing MacNabb, but leaving the man to suffer, knowing what had been done to his daughter, how she'd suffered before she died, would be worth it.

A FEW HOURS LATER, AFTER SITTING IN ON SOME OF THE LAIRDS' gathering, Tavish crossed the bailey headed for the stables to let the stable master know the lairds planned to go hunting the day after tomorrow. Yvaine was talking to the man, Kilgore, who'd been with her and her father at the midday meal. Now, she was walking in the bailey with him and, apparently, showing him around. As if she knew the Aerie like her own home. Perhaps she did, in a way, if her father had told her much about it.

Tavish did his best to keep an eye on Yvaine, but he had

duties of his own, including responding to his laird's demands. He didn't like the thought of leaving her with that man, but after having seen her and her father with Kilgore, he realized he could have been wrong about him. Yet she'd said she met him here. And her father knew that. Tavish shook his head. He needed to talk to Donal. In the meantime, Yvaine was in full view of the guards on the battlements, as well as in the midst of people crossing the bailey. She should be safe long enough for him to take care of his father's errand, though leaving her worried him.

Then he spotted Bhaltair, across the bailey, watching her. Nay, his gaze was on Kilgore. And as they moved deeper into the keep, Tavish saw Bhaltair signal one of his men to follow them. Relieved, Tavish pulled his gaze from Yvaine and entered the stable.

Did she know the Aerie's secrets? That thought chilled him. Surely, even if she did, she would not share them with a strange guardsman.

Then again, one never knew what a lass would do.

He vowed to keep a closer eye on her. He'd promised her mother he would, and despite knowing Yvaine would not welcome his escort, he wanted to. But perhaps he should also enlist Eilidh to befriend her and keep her busy. Then again, Eilidh had her hands full helping their mother stay ready to tend to the injuries that could be sustained by their many visitors, so perhaps not.

His twin had already remarked that she'd never seen such an accident-prone group as the one now inhabiting the glen. Boredom was more likely the culprit. With nothing more to do than wait for their lairds to call on their services, men would train and be injured; drink too much, fight and be injured; ride in races, fall from their horses and be injured; and a host of other reasons. She claimed to have seen it all since the bulk of the visitors arrived. For men here to guard their lairds, they seemed little intent on doing their jobs and more intent on competitions of all sorts. All leading to injuries.

Was it some sort of competition that had led to Donal's injury? Some contest he'd gotten in the way of. An accident, as Donal had said? Bhaltair was close-mouthed on the subject, but to Tavish, he seemed grim and determined. Never a good sign in anyone, but in a man with his reputation? Tavish shuddered. They thought they'd caught the man who'd hurled the blade, but the men around him swore he could not have done it. Bhaltair let him go, but Tavish was certain the man and his friends would be watched closely. Along with the MacKyrie guards who'd come with their laird and her family, there were more Lathan guards down in the glen today than there had been any day before now. He hoped they would prove able to keep the men there under control, and perhaps find the man who'd—deliberately or by accident—threatened Donal's life. Unless he was already in the Aerie with Yvaine.

When Tavish finished with the stable master, he returned to the bailey, but Yvaine and her companion had disappeared. Perhaps they'd gone back into the keep. Dark clouds were massing to the west. There would be rain tonight, possibly a storm. If Kilgore had a tent in the glen, best he get down there and make it secure.

Tavish walked the bailey just in case Yvaine was in trouble. His dreams had stopped once he met her in person, but he still suffered the sense of foreboding that had begun with the visions. He didn't find her, so he went back into the keep, knowing Bhaltair had men protecting her, and hoping she'd had sense enough to go back inside before the storm hit.

There! Crossing the great hall by herself, headed for the hearthside where her mother sat with his.

Relieved, Tavish headed for the kitchen to advise the cook about the hunt. Food and drink would be needed early that morning, as well as supplies the men could take with them.

When he came back to the great hall, the women still sat where he'd last seen them. He returned to the laird's solar to report to his father and see what else he needed, shared a quick supper with him, then headed to his chamber for some much-needed rest.

TAVISH WAS FLOATING, DRIFTING AGAIN, WITH NO CONTROL OVER HIS *movements. He looked toward the Aerie's gate, then back the other way, deeper into the bailey. He couldn't see anyone. Where was the lass?*

Then he moved faster, still with the odd floating motion, so familiar in this strange place.

There. Yvaine. He was not alone. She walked away from him, her russet dress rippling with her movement, her brown hair swaying down her back with each step as it always did. Left. Right. He followed the swing of her hair. She glanced back over her shoulder and smiled at him. He stood, frozen with desire, cold and hot at the same time. How could she hate him in the real world and smile at him here?

When she looked away, Tavish tried to call out to her, but he couldn't make a sound. Instead, he floated after her until she disappeared around the side of the kirk. Fear replaced the burning desire that drove him after her. Where had she gone?

For the first time since the visions involving her started, he rounded the corner of the kirk. He halted, horror roiling his belly. He squeezed his eyes shut, then opened them again, praying the vision would change. She was still there. But she was on the ground, that gorgeous bronze hair wrapped around her long, graceful neck. Graceful no more, it bent at an unnatural angle. Her sightless eyes gazed up at him as if begging him to save her.

He was too late.

11

He woke.

It was morning. Tavish sat up, heart pounding and head throbbing, praying this vision was not real. The last vestiges of the dream still clouded his mind and ruled his body, the sensations much stronger than any previous dream. He feared this time, he'd dreamed true. His shock and fury at seeing her lifeless body on the ground battled for supremacy in his muscles, alternately tightening them and leaving him weak and shaky.

If ever he'd been wrong about a Seeing, he hoped he was wrong about this one.

If he was right, the lass he'd met only a few days ago—the daughter of one of his father's oldest friends—would die here, in the Aerie, and he would not be able to save her.

The storm Tavish had expected last evening rumbled outside his window. Had a crash of thunder woken him up? He clenched his fist. If he'd remained in the vision, would he have seen who killed his dream Yvaine? Tavish collapsed back into his pillow in a cold sweat and ground the heels of his hands into his eyes. After having no dreams about her since he'd met her, his dream had returned with a vengeance, and with a dire message.

Her mother's intervention had worked, it seemed, to sharpen his talent and strengthen it. If the stakes were not so high for Yvaine, he'd wish her mother's intervention had failed. He'd gone from foreboding to seeing her dead.

How was he to protect a lass who didn't want to be protected? A lass, who, as the daughter of Donal MacNabb, believed herself untouchable. Even invincible. How could he convince her to accept him at her side? And to do it without telling her he'd seen her death.

He couldn't imagine how she'd react to that news. Would she believe him? Did she have enough faith in her mother's talent not to question his? Or, knowing that her mother had been asked to help him strengthen his talent, would she laugh off his dream as just that. A dream, and not a Seeing.

Her mother! Had she seen anything yet? Surely she must have. Why would Tavish be the only Seer to be shown that her daughter was in deadly danger? Her husband, too, if one accepted that his injury yesterday was not the accident Donal had told Yvaine it was. Why then was Yvaine not locked away somewhere safe? The only answer that made sense was that the MacKyrie Seer must not have had any visions about her daughter.

He had to find one of them. Ellie or Yvaine. He had to warn them. Someone was determined to kill MacKyries. Even Ellie could be in danger. If he told his father or Donal, they might laugh off his warnings. He needed to appeal to the Seer. She would understand and believe him.

He glanced toward the window. Despite the dark clouds overhead, he didn't hear rain, and he could tell the sun was well up. There was too much activity in the bailey for the hour to be as early as the vestiges of storm clouds made it seem. He'd slept much later than usual, caught in the throes of his vision. Yvaine might be in the great hall breaking her fast. Or with her mother, in his mother's herbal. He threw on his clothes, pulled on his boots, tucked his dirk in his belt and left his chamber, moving quickly, the urgency of his dream still driving him.

He met Yvaine as she was coming up the stairs, near the top. He would rather have this conversation with her mother, but Yvaine was standing in front of him. "Come with me," he told her without first bothering to greet her politely. He grasped her arm, and hurried her up the last few steps with him.

"Let go of me!" She punched at his hand with her free hand. "What do ye think ye are doing?"

"Trying to keep ye safe. Damn it, Yvaine," he growled as she landed a blow to his ribs. "Stop that. We have to talk."

"I don't have to talk to ye or do anything else. Ye embarrassed the life out of me yesterday and here ye are, dragging me about again."

That stopped him. "I apologized. As did ye. I thought we were past that." At her derisive sniff, he turned and grasped her other arm, then held her still before him. "I have *seen* it, Yvaine. Again and again. And 'tis getting worse. Ye are in danger."

"The only danger I'm in is from ye."

"Yet ye apologized to me yesterday. Or was that just for yer da's benefit?"

She looked away.

"Well, ye are wrong. I willna harm ye. But someone wants to."

"Ye are harming me right now. I'll have bruises on both my arms."

He eased up the pressure but didn't let go. She tried to jerk away from him and he shook his head. "Come with me. I must tell ye what I've seen." But could he tell her all of it? He escorted her down the hall to her chamber, opened the door and motioned for her to precede him. "Go on in."

She tried to close the door in his face, but he was too quick.

He shoved the door open. It sent her sprawling onto her back-side on the floor. "Damn ye!" Her cry came out from between gritted teeth, her lips compressed into an angry line. Fury sparked in her eyes.

He closed the door, then bent to help her up. "I'm sorry. I didna mean for that to happen."

She batted his hand away. "Do *not* touch me," she snarled, got to her feet and moved to the window. "Say what ye want to say, then get out. Ye shouldna be in here. If my Da kenned, we'd both be in trouble." She held out a hand, palm forward, warning him off. "And if ye come near me, I'll scream. Everyone in the bailey will hear me."

He leaned back against the door, giving her the space she demanded. "The dream I told ye about yesterday at the gate. Before—"

"Before my da was attacked, aye. Ye seemed not to be surprised by that."

"What? I was, as much as ye." He ran a hand through his hair, then slid down the door to squat at its base, rested his arms on his knees and turned up open hands. "Why do ye think so badly of me, Yvaine. I'm trying to help ye."

"It doesna seem like it." She rubbed her arms.

"I said I'm sorry. I am," he reminded her, appalled that he'd hurt her yet again. It didn't seem possible to have so much trouble with one lass, but he appeared to be fated to do just that.

She *hmphed* but said nothing else.

"The dream I told ye about yesterday. I had it for weeks before I met ye. The same every night. With a strong sense of foreboding. Something wrong. Some danger I couldna see. I could only see ye. For weeks, I've followed ye and tried to reach ye, to find out why ye were there. But the vision wouldna let me touch ye."

She rolled her eyes. "That sounds preferable to me."

"'Tisna, Yvaine. I got closer and closer. Last night..." He paused. How much to tell her? "Last night I saw ye in trouble. I mean to keep ye safe, lass. There's more to this than dreaming of danger ahead."

Something in his tone, in his eyes, must have gotten through to her. She frowned and opened her mouth, then hesitated. Finally, she raised a hand. "I had much the same for my Da. Never a vision, but an ache of foreboding in my belly. What did ye see? What does it mean?"

Tavish took a breath. *Now* she was curious? At least she no longer seemed intent on fighting with him. Wait, what? "Ye never dreamed of yer da? Are ye a Seer, too?"

"Ye ken my mother. What makes ye think I would be anything else?"

Tavish leaned his head against the door, lifted it and knocked it back again several times, trying to pound some sense into it. How could he be so stupid? Of course, she was a Seer. "And ye have seen naught about danger to yerself?"

She canted her head. "Do ye ever have visions about yer own future?"

"Nay, not so far."

"Nor I. Nor any my mother has mentioned about herself. I dinna think it works that way."

"Has she seen what ye have about yer da?"

"She has not, but she was drinking a sleeping potion for her pain. And mine are not always reliable, much as ye said about yers. We were never certain."

"I fear ye can be certain of mine. They have repeated too often, too much the same, to be anything but warnings."

Yvaine left the window and took his hand, urging him up from the floor. If she hadn't spent years listening to her mother's tales, she might never believe Tavish's. But she had. She must believe him. The emotion in his voice and in his eyes told her he sincerely believed what he was telling her. And after the way he apologized and stood up to her da for making her a laughingstock when he ordered Tavish to carry her back up the tor, she had begun to trust him. She could give him the benefit of the doubt on this, even if his talent was as untested and possibly unreliable as her own. "I ken ye believe that. But Mother hasna seen..."

"The sleeping draught must still prevent her—"

"Or she's had dreams she doesna recall. Or canna interpret. Even for an experienced Seer, many visions are cloaked in symbols." Those were the only possibilities that made sense to Yvaine.

Tavish groaned. "God's bones, dinna tell me that. I had hoped my talent would become stronger and clearer over time. It canna remain this unpredictable forever."

Yvaine crossed her arms and paced away from him, then back again to face him. "I feel the same way. So, what have ye seen that ye havena told me?"

Tavish reached out and brushed a lock of hair from her cheek. "I really am trying to help ye. And I dinna want to frighten ye with the rest until I speak to yer mother."

"Too late," she groaned. "What can be worse than not kenning?"

"Trust me a little longer," he told her. "Please."

She sighed and dropped her shoulders, fighting the urge to lean her face into his hand. She hadn't realized how tense she was until that moment. Nor how inviting Tavish's nearness had become, once she accepted his sincerity. How warm he seemed, both in body and in spirit. How good he smelled. Her very senses betrayed her into wanting him even nearer. She wanted to feel those strong arms of his wrap around her and hold her close. But she dared not give in to the urge. "Very well. I believe ye, and I will let ye speak to mother first, if that is what ye feel ye must do. Now, what do we do about all of this?"

"I must stay near ye. Escort ye. Ye canna wander about alone with strange men from the glen."

Normally, she'd berate him for trying to control whom she made friends with, but given the tale he told, she accepted his concern was sincere. "Iver is not a strange man. He's a clan chief's guard or he wouldna be here."

"That's what he said. That is not what I observed. I saw him acting strangely soon after the lairds arrived. He might have been following yer da toward the stables several nights ago. I stopped him before he could get close. I dinna think yer da kenned he was there."

Her stomach sank. Had Tavish saved her father's life? Before she could ask, he continued.

"He tried to associate with the MacBean in the solar. I saw that laird arrive. He swore he brought only the two men I saw arrive with him. Yer friend wasna one of them."

The hollow in her belly spread to her chest.

"Listen to me, Yvaine," Tavish continued despite her expression. "I think he lied to ye. He means to get close to ye, probably as a way to get to yer father. By harming ye in order to hurt him. Has he tried...anything with ye?"

She rubbed her arms where Tavish gripped them. "He hasna hurt me." She watched him like a mouse watched a cat as he stepped closer to her.

"Has he tried to touch ye in any way ye didna like?"

She looked up and met his gaze, scowling. Did he think another man would not be attracted to her? That her only enticement was as a way to approach her da?

"Nay, nor would I let him."

"Good. I want ye to stay away from him."

"Ye canna tell me what to do."

"I have seen ye in danger, Yvaine. I have seen ye harmed. I

will do anything in my power to keep my visions from coming true."

"Tell me what ye have seen."

The haunted look in Tavish's eyes as he considered her demand made Yvaine's belly tighten.

"I told ye what I can," he finally said and turned away from her.

She had been shocked to hear that he'd seen her in dreams for weeks before they met, not just a few days. "So ye follow me," she repeated back to him, "coming closer each time, but never reaching me as I walk away from ye, turn a corner and disappear." Baffled, she told him, "That means nothing to me. Perhaps ye need to...direct the dream somehow. Reach me and keep me from turning the corner, from disappearing."

"I could hope the dream doesna imply danger at all," he said, still facing away from her, "but something between us that is just out of reach, something that we strive for." That haunted look was back in his eyes.

"I dinna ken if it could mean something as benign as that, not with the foreboding ye feel." She shook her head. "Tell me the truth, Tavish. I am strong enough to accept it."

"Are ye? Then I must hope it means ye will accept this." He stepped closer, caressed her cheek, then ran his fingers through her hair and caressed her nape. God's teeth, the tingles his touch set off ran down her body and gathered in her core. Her eyes closed and her head fell back.

Apparently, he could not resist the temptation she offered. He bent his head, whispered a breath over her lips as he groaned her name, and kissed her.

She stilled for a moment, shocked at the sensation of his firm lips brushing hers. His touch was all she'd imagined, and more. Her body responded before she could deny the urge. Her lips parted on a surprised exhale and she rose on her toes to meet his kiss, to inhale his scent, to thread her fingers in his hair. He called to her in a way she didn't understand, but that made her want more. She didn't know what that more would be. Only that he tasted...irresistible.

He groaned. His kiss turned even more heated, more demanding, forcing her head back and her mouth open as his arms wrapped around her and pulled her tightly against him. He traced the inside of her lower lip with his tongue, then gently sucked her lip into his mouth and used his tongue to tease a moan from her. She'd never expected to be kissed like that. What else did she not know? And what kind of risk was she taking in letting Tavish show her?

She jerked back. What was she thinking, letting him kiss her at all? Letting him touch her and—nay! She dropped her hands from his neck and pushed off his shoulders and out of his arms. "What do ye think ye are doing?" She marched to the opposite side of the room, then turned to make certain he hadn't followed her. He still stood by the door. Relief made her drop onto the window seat.

"I apologize," he said softly.

He was as breathless as she. That made her feel somehow powerful, which made no sense. She'd been helpless in his arms, lost in the swirl of unfamiliar sensations his kiss made her feel. He had not been helpless at all. He'd done exactly what he wanted to do.

She summoned that new sense of power, sat up straighter and met his gaze.

"I couldna resist ye, Yvaine. I've seen ye in my dreams for so long..." He reached out a hand, then dropped it. "Each time ye turned and gazed at me with just a hint of a smile, I hoped it might mean ye would grow to feel something for me."

"That makes nay sense. Ye have said yer vision fills ye with foreboding. Where is the danger in my glance?" She touched her lips. "This, what we just did, has naught to do with yer vision."

"I—ye dinna ken what ye are capable of. What ye do to me."

"Nay, Tavish. I think ye imagine some unseen danger in yer vision just as ye imagine I might grow to feel something for ye." She crossed her arms. "Yer vision doesna foretell danger for me. The only danger I am in is from ye." She pointed to the door. "Ye must leave."

"Nay, lass. I willna kiss ye again. I must..."

"Nay, ye willna. And ye mustna do anything save get out of my chamber, now." When he didn't move, she added, "Before I start screaming."

He opened his mouth, closed it, then finally said, "Dinna do that. I'll go." He looked past her to the open window that gave out onto the bailey.

His dismay was evident in the way his shoulders suddenly drooped. He lost his normally proud bearing. She found his willingness to take her seriously, and do as she asked, endearing. Endearing? Ach, nay. He was a danger to her.

"Go on. I dinna want ye here."

"But ye need me here."

"Nay, I dinna. I'll lock the door. Ye can stand guard in the hallway if ye feel the need. And ye can explain to my da, when he returns to the chamber across the hall, why ye are there. I hope ye can make up a better reason than what ye told me of yer visions before he gets here."

"I didna tell ye all, Yvaine. I canna. I dinna ken if 'tis real."

"There is more? Ye must tell me."

"Nay." He looked even more defeated. "I'll go speak to yer mother—or yer da. Whomever I find first." He paused at the open door and turned back to her. "Yvaine, please. Bolt the door. Dinna open it for anyone save me, yer mother or yer father. 'Tis important."

"I'll not be made a prisoner in this chamber." She shuddered, recalling her father had threatened her with that. Dear

God, with all of Tavish's talk of danger to her, would her da follow through?

"I dinna mean for ye to remain here for long. Only to keep ye safe until I can return. We'll go down to the great hall later to supper and sit with our families, together. There will be plenty of Lathan guards in the hall."

"Enough that ye willna need to remain beside me? Perfect." She pointed to the door. "Now go." She didn't know what he thought she'd do until then, but she didn't intend to remain locked in here for the rest of the day—or of the gathering. She would find somewhere to go. Perhaps Eilidh...nay, Tavish's twin would have to tell her parents where she was. She crossed her arms, willing Tavish to leave so she could think.

Much to her relief, after a moment he spent studying her, possibly assessing her resolve, he nodded and left.

Tavish had known he was about to make a big mistake. It didn't take a Seer's talent to tell him that giving in to his urge to kiss Yvaine would complicate an already impossible situation. But being with her, near her, and not fighting with her, made his desire for her surge to the forefront. Yvaine, being cooperative, understanding, sharing his insecurities and finding she had the same, had been more than his need for her could resist. He couldn't help himself.

He'd kissed her. He'd enjoyed every moment of feeling her in his arms, her lush, pink lips warm and moist beneath his. Her scent. Everything about her seemed made to lure him closer and closer until there was no turning back.

And then she pulled away from him.

And ran near that damn window again.

She might think she'd managed to get rid of him, but after he spoke to her mother, and if need be, to Donal MacNabb himself, she'd find out differently. He'd started this with good intentions, simply to protect her. After tasting her lips, feeling her lush body in his arms, both yesterday and today, he meant to have her. To keep her. To make her his.

But first, he had to protect her. To save her—even from himself, for now—if he hoped she would ever accept him.

How to do it? He'd avoided telling her all he'd seen. But her demands to leave her alone left him in a quandary. He couldn't tell her he'd seen her with her hair wrapped around her lifeless throat. He wouldn't frighten her that way. So how to make her take her danger seriously and accept him?

He needed help. Her parents, aye. And his. And Eilidh, if that's what it took to keep Lathan eyes on her at all times. Bhaltair, certainly. He'd kept the import of his visions to himself for too long. Her father had been attacked. And a stranger was sniffing around her. Tavish would not allow that to continue. He was all for Yvaine being able to choose her friends, but not here. Not now. Not after he'd seen her dead.

He went across the hall and knocked softly on the MacKyrie door. No answer. Donal was probably in the solar with the other lairds. Ellie might be there as well, or with his mother in her herbal.

He went there next.

He heard their laughter even before he reached the door to the herbal. Both women were sitting at their ease, platters of food and drink at their elbows on tables his mother normally used to chop up herbs for various preparations. He and his siblings had always been strictly forbidden from bringing food into this room, much less eating at one of her preparation tables.

She noticed him enter and frown at the table where they sat. "*Dinna fash*, Tavish. The last things I minced here were parsley and mint. Naught dangerous at all. What can I do for ye?"

He cleared his throat and glanced from her to Ellie MacKyrie, who studied him with unusual intensity, and back again.

"There's something I've seen. Something I must tell ye and beg yer forgiveness that I didna tell ye sooner. And beg yer assistance..."

"'Tis about Yvaine, is it not?" Ellie swung around to face him, then glanced aside at his mother. "Tell me." She was calm, her voice even, yet commanding. The laird had spoken, as well as the mother.

He nodded and steeled himself for what he must reveal. "Ye ken I've been having dreams. Visions with a strong sense of foreboding. The same each night for weeks before ye arrived." He had described them, but this time, he was going to have to tell them about the latest vision. "After I met Yvaine, the dreams...ceased."

Ellie's eyes widened briefly, but she said nothing, so he continued. "As if meeting her was the point of the visions. The message. But after our session," he added, looking at the Seer, "I had another. If my talent has strengthened and has revealed more to me, the vision I had last night is the result."

Both women began speaking at once. Aileana paused to let the Seer speak. Ellie wasted no time getting to the point. "What did ye see?"

Tavish was still torn. He knew he had to tell Yvaine's mother. He'd come here to do that. But how to tell her without upsetting her? He looked from her to his own mother. She nodded in that sage way she had when it seemed she could read his mind. She would help him, no matter what he needed.

Instead of immediately revealing what he'd seen, he asked the Seer a question. "Have ye had any visions? Any that have to do with either yer husband or yer daughter? Yvaine has been fashed about danger to her da."

"Which came true yesterday when he was stabbed," Aileana said.

"Perhaps," Ellie replied. "Or perhaps that was just a warning. To answer ye, Tavish, nay, I havena. Yer mother tells me my visions should return soon. My body is still under the influence of the valerian I used for long weeks against my pain. Yer mother has eliminated its cause. I no longer need the tisane. Best ye warn me, lad. What am I likely to see?"

Tavish inclined his head, silently asking forgiveness before he spoke. "Yer daughter, Laird MacKyrie, strangled with her own hair somewhere in the Aerie. Dead."

"Dear God." Aileana's exclamation hissed out between her teeth. She grasped Ellie's shoulder and tensed. Closing her eyes, she breathed deeply, several times, until the Seer was able to mimic her and do the same.

Ellie had paled, but Aileana's touch returned some color to her face. "Have ye told her?" That was her mother speaking, concern in every syllable.

"She kens all except that last. I...couldna tell her. Why frighten her with a vision I've seen only once—one that might not be a true seeing?"

"Ye ken better than that," Aileana said, her voice firm with conviction.

"Aye, I do, though 'tis hard to accept."

"She must be guarded," Ellie said softly. "I ken we talked about this already, but now 'tis even more important. Tavish, will ye stay by my daughter?" The plea in her eyes tore at him as much as the entreaty in her voice. "Aileana, can he be spared? Can Lathan provide men to watch over her? Or shall I call up the rest of my men from the glen?"

"He can," she said firmly. "And so can others, including MacKyries, if ye wish. Though yer husband and mine have assigned yer men to help find the man who stabbed Donal."

"And since they are already based in the glen, they attract less notice than yer men," Ellie agreed. "Very well." She turned to Tavish. "I must depend on ye and Lathan guards. Can I?"

"I will guard your daughter, Laird MacKyrie, gladly, but I fear Yvaine will still not accept me by her side."

"Why not?" This time, her voice rang out, sharp and clear.

"She has resented my attempts to this point to keep her safe. She does not know the content of my latest vision, only that I have seen her in danger and have reason to fear for her."

"She will do as she's told or her da will lock her away. She kens fine that he does not speak lightly when he makes promises. He promised to do just that, should she be found to be in danger." She stopped and took another breath, then stood. "I must speak to him." She glanced around at Aileana. "I presume he's with the other lairds?"

"So far as I ken," she answered.

"And my daughter, where is she?"

"I left her in her chamber. With the door locked from the inside," he told her.

"Where I hope she's had sense enough to remain."

"I told her I'd return to take her down to supper later, and that we would sit with both families."

"Good thinking." She nodded, then added after a glance at his mother, "Aye, ye will do nicely."

"For what?"

"Go check on her, will ye, please?"

Tavish knew a distraction when his mother used one. She didn't intend for Ellie to answer his question. He narrowed his eyes at her to warn her that he knew what she was up to, and left the herbal. He didn't need his mother, or worse, both of their mothers, pairing them together, planning a betrothal and a wedding. Not when Yvaine could not abide him. Though she had kissed him back. He would agree readily to a match, but convincing her would take more time than he probably had— in this lifetime. Whatever happened between them must happen at their pace, not their mothers'.

He was tempted to pause outside the door and listen in case

they continued to converse and in the course of it, explained the Seer's cryptic remark that he would *do*. In case he was mistaken. But no doubt his mother would know full well that he was out here. Instead, he made some noise as he went down the hallway toward the great hall, greeted cook as he passed by the door to the kitchen and generally acted as he would have if he was still twelve years old and bent on convincing his mother he was innocent of something he'd actually done. Only now, he wasn't guilty of anything.

Nay, he was.

He'd kissed Yvaine. He'd wanted more. And she had seemed, for a few moments, to have wanted the same. Wanted his kiss. Even wanted him. Before she came to her senses and pulled away.

She was going to be a challenge. But she didn't know who she was dealing with. From his family, and probably, from hers, he would have more help than she could imagine or resist.

As he crossed the great hall, he was caught as the lairds spilled out of his father's solar, taking a midday break from their discussions. His father called him to sit with several of the lairds and keep them entertained. Tavish held up a hand when he spotted Donal, telling his father he'd be with him in a moment. "Donal, yer wife needs to speak with ye. She's in Mother's herbal. 'Tis important."

Donal didn't argue, he simply nodded and left the great hall.

Since Yvaine was safely behind a locked door in her chamber, and her parents were discussing what to do about Tavish's latest vision, he'd done all he could for now. So why was his belly still tight? Without giving his father the details in the middle of the crowded great hall, Tavish tried to convince him that he was needed elsewhere, but Toran gave him no choice. Tavish did as his father and laird bid and broke his fast while he talked with two lairds he'd only met the day before.

Two hours passed before he was able to escape, his gut churning and the back of his neck prickling the entire time. Had Yvaine's parents gone to speak with her? To tell her what Tavish had seen and convince her to remain in her chamber, under guard? He hoped Yvaine had obeyed and stayed safe where he'd left her long enough for her parents to arrive. She was suspicious of him and stubbornly independent. He suspected her first impulse would be to disobey, but his warnings—and the kiss they'd shared—might have been enough to make her want to stay put just to avoid him. As he climbed the stairs, he chided himself for his musings.

He went first to her parents' chamber. If they wanted something other than what Yvaine's mother had asked of him, he should know before he talked to her. No one answered, so he went across the hall to Yvaine's chamber.

He knocked on the door, fully expecting her parents to still be inside with her. "'Tis me," he called out. "Yvaine? Open the door."

Receiving no answer, he tried the handle, not surprised when the door opened easily. His belly sank.

Damn her. She'd left her chamber, and he had no idea where she was now.

12

Dark clouds still filled the sky, making the afternoon feel like dusk, which fell early this time of year. The gloom suited Yvaine perfectly. After Tavish's revelations, she would not stay in that chamber another minute, especially when she expected her father's next act would be to lock her inside and post guards outside her door to prevent her from leaving.

This might be her last chance to slip out through the great hall before the laird's gathering ended and wander at will around the bailey. All the men, even the one Tavish suspected, would be involved in the gathering or guarding the gathering. Or he would be down in the glen in a tent, planning his next move. Either way, she doubted he would be in the bailey, waiting for her.

For now, she was in no danger. If Tavish and her father had their way, all she would see from now on was the four walls of her chamber and the view from her chamber's window. The thought made her want to weep. She could circumvent Tavish, but could she do the same to her father? Never. Her freedom of movement was about to be curtailed. She'd best take advantage while she could.

She visited the puppies first. They were still adorable, in the way of all baby animals. She spent longer than she'd intended to, but found it hard to leave their happy company. Stable lads passed by a few times, but other than asking if she needed anything, they left her alone. The puppies played about her feet, then jumped on her lap when she knelt in clean straw to pet them. "I'm sorry," she told them. "I didna think to bring anything to feed ye." Their mother watched from nearby, apparently glad to have someone distract them and give her a few minutes rest. Thoroughly licked by small, wet tongues attached to wriggly, warm and squeaking bodies, Yvaine finally stood and left the young family.

She walked past the smithy where one man still pounded on something and made her ears ring. She continued on to the weavers' workrooms. No one was there, but while she had sufficient daylight to do so, she stopped to admire the half-finished cloth on their looms. Then, as darkness began to thicken and creep across the ground and up the walls of the bailey, she made her way to the kirk.

Silence and peace descended on her as she took a seat. For long minutes, she simply sat and enjoyed her solitude and the sense of calm reflection the space gave her. Then she looked around. The kirk was small, even intimate, obviously a family space for the Lathans and their retainers. She imagined feast days and high holy days would have to be celebrated with the double doors opened wide for people outside to take part. That seemed lovely and welcoming. Did they have a resident priest? No one had greeted her when she came inside. Perhaps if they did, the friar had gone to the great hall for the evening meal.

With that thought, her stomach rumbled. It was time for her to do the same. Tavish would return to her chamber soon and she would be missed. Her father would be livid. She said a small prayer for freedom and salvation, then left the kirk, closing the doors softly behind her.

No sooner had she turned the corner into the gap between the kirk and the stone wall than a man grabbed her from behind. She sucked in air to scream. He slapped one hand over her mouth and growled into her ear, "Make a sound and ye'll be dead instead of swived."

Her scream died in her throat. She jerked against his hold, twisted and kicked. He was too strong and too big. She couldn't escape him.

Did she recognize his voice? She couldn't be sure. If only she could see him, she could describe him...after. Nay, she wouldn't think about what he wanted to do. She'd stop him somehow. She'd prayed for freedom and salvation, never expecting she'd need divine help this soon.

She fought for all she was worth, managing to bite the hand that muzzled her. He swore and threw her to the ground, then his knee on the small of her back held her down while one hand kept her head down. The other hand, she realized with horror, was pulling up her skirts. She struggled, but her efforts seemed only to amuse him.

He chuckled, infuriating her and making her struggle harder.

Cold air hit the skin above her hose on the back of her thighs. Dear God, he was going to do this. She bit back a sob and kicked. His grunt told her she'd connected. She kicked again.

He pushed her head harder into the dirt. "Keep that up and I'll smother ye," he threatened.

She clawed at the hand on her head. He swore. Heartened, she bucked, trying to unbalance him. Her eating knife was in its scabbard on her belt—underneath her. If she could get to it, she might make him regret this.

Suddenly, the man was gone.

She rolled to her side and pulled her small blade.

Two men fought nearby in the darkness. She couldn't

mistake the thud of fists on flesh or the grunts and hisses as blows landed. If one was her attacker, who was her rescuer? The light was too dim to make out any details. They were too close to the keep's outer wall for torchlight from the battlements to reach here.

As she sat up, she shoved her skirts back down her legs, then stood, brandishing her wee blade. She glanced around, looking for a way to escape, but the fighters were too close for her to get by them and run for the keep. A sharp cry quickly pulled her gaze back to the men. Were they coming closer? Her only option was the kirk, but inside, with the doors shut and no way to bar them, she'd be at the mercy of the next man to enter. The thought of being trapped there made her stomach climb up into her throat. Nay, she had to get past them.

Or there was another way to save herself.

She screamed as loudly as she could. And screamed again. If her attacker was winning, she would soon need help.

Her screams must have startled the men. Suddenly, one of them jerked free and ran away. Damn the moon's feeble glow. It was too dark to see more than his shape.

The man who'd fought with him took a step to follow, watched for a moment as if debating chasing him, then turned to her. "Yvaine, did he hurt ye?"

That voice, she knew. "Tavish! How did ye find me?"

"I've been looking for ye for more than an hour." He held out a hand to her.

She took it and let him pull her to him.

"Ye were supposed to stay in yer chamber."

She heard the bite in his voice, the same bite she'd heard the day she ran down the tor to her injured father. Once again, she'd made him angry. Nay, furious.

"Thank ye for finding me. Ye came just in time."

"So instead of remaining in yer chamber where ye were safe, ye'd rather a stranger ravish ye? Kill ye?"

Her heart skipped a beat. Tavish was not mollified. And the man had threatened to do both. Numbly, she shook her head.

"I thought not. Are ye harmed in any way?"

"Bruised perhaps. He didna have time..."

"Good," he snapped, then more softly said, "Yer screams may have drawn out some men from the great hall or the wall walk. They can hunt for yer attacker. Come, I'll take ye to mother and let her make sure ye are well."

"Nay, dinna bother her."

He tugged on her hand, pulling her along with him. "Ye have to be the most stubborn lass I've ever had the misfortune to meet. For once, can ye just do as ye are told? For yer own good?"

"Let go of me." She yanked her hand free and stopped, hands on hips. "Ye warned me something like this might happen. Because ye kenned it would? Why didna ye tell me it would happen today?"

She knew her accusations were unfounded and unfair, but she was shaking and needed to lash out at someone. Tavish had made himself a convenient target.

"I didna know it would happen today. I've done naught but warn ye, Yvaine. Ye dinna want to believe me. Why do ye think so little of me?" He took her arm and hurried her toward the keep's stout door.

"Because every time something happens to me, ye are there. Why would I not suspect ye?"

He stopped and put his hands on her shoulders. Gently, this time. Perhaps he was thinking back to the last time he had handled her more roughly. "I'm trying to keep ye safe, Yvaine. 'Tis all I've ever tried to do. I care about ye. Why can ye not understand that?"

"Why? Because trouble follows ye."

"Nay, lass. Trouble is following ye."

Before supper, Aileana pronounced Yvaine well enough to have her meal. Both families headed for the great hall. Tavish took a seat next to his twin. His parents sat at the head table with Drummond and his wife, Morven, then Eilidh, and him. He left Yvaine in the care of her parents, sitting at a table nearest his family's.

Toran Lathan's countenance was as angry as his wife's was calm. He would be furious that the attack on Yvaine had happened in his keep to one of his guests and worse, to the daughter of one of his closest friends. Aileana would be pleased that Yvaine had escaped mostly unharmed, and that she had been able to quickly mend the bruises Yvaine complained of. Both, Tavish suspected, were vastly relieved that he had arrived in time to save Yvaine from greater harm, but both fathers would be spoiling to know who her attacker was. They knew how he'd gotten away. In his fear for Yvaine, Tavish had let him go. He regretted that now. He could have ended the danger to her tonight, but he'd failed to do so. They didn't know if her attacker had been the man they suspected, Kilgore, or someone else, taking advantage of a lass alone in the dark. He hadn't been found yet.

Donal MacNabb looked ready to explode and kept shooting angry glances at his daughter. On her other side, her mother talked to her, low and soft. He almost wished he could hear what she told Yvaine. Almost.

Every time Donal MacNabb's frown lanced his way, Tavish fervently regretted he'd been unable to restrain the man, but his concern had been to get to Yvaine as quickly as he could. She could have been injured and bleeding—or worse. He knew she was alive when he pulled the man off of her, but that was all he'd had time to notice.

He turned away from the MacKyries. He'd deliberately

chosen the seat as far from Yvaine as he could get while still keeping his promise that they would sup with their families. But given the tension inhabiting them all, even here was too close.

Eilidh, normally quiet and shy, smirked in his direction. "Ye seem to have ruined yer chances with that lass," she teased.

"I never had any," he groused. "Even after I saved her life, she blames me for everything that has happened to her since she arrived here. What am I doing wrong?"

"Perhaps ye need to back off. Take it slow."

"There's no time to take things slow," he complained. "At best, the gathering ends and they leave. At worse, my vision comes to pass and she dies—"

"What?" Eilidh kept her squeal low, but gripped his hand, wide-eyed, her shock evident. "What have ye seen, brother?"

"Yvaine. Dead. I may have kept that from happening tonight, but neither of us got a good look at her attacker. He could try again. I have to stay close to her, one way or the other."

"I would imagine Da will assign Bhaltair that duty. Does she ken?"

"Nay, but her parents do. And ours. I told them earlier today."

"What took ye so long?"

He pursed his lips. "Ye ken how unreliable my visions are."

"Ye have been having the same one for weeks. That seems fair reliable to me."

"Until this last one where I saw her dead."

Eilidh touched his hand. "I dinna envy ye, brother."

"Nor I ye, taking everyone else's pain."

"The good thing about pain is that ye forget it. Else men would never fight again, and women would never have more than one bairn. But the things ye see in yer visions can stay with ye forever."

Tavish let her comment roll off him. "She needs a companion. A lass who can be in the chamber with her."

Eilidh held up her hand. "Ye ken I canna. Mother needs me."

"And 'tis not proper for me to take on that duty."

"Ye could bed down across her doorway."

"So, someone could stab me in my sleep, then step over me to get to her? I never have understood the logic of that idea."

"I suppose it depends on how heavily ye sleep."

"During a vision? Very. I'd be useless. Then dead."

"Then she'll have one of Bhaltair's men at her door, and ye can stop fashing over her."

Tavish didn't like that idea. He'd sworn to protect her. Aye, more guards would help, but she was his responsibility. Even though she'd tried to reject him, he'd promised her. And her mother, the MacKyrie laird. Somehow, he had to do it.

AFTER SUPPER, TORAN TOOK TAVISH ASIDE. "DONAL WILL BRING up some of his men from the glen, but he has asked that ye serve as Yvaine's personal guard. Given what happened this evening, I think 'tis wise that she be escorted. It doesna have to be ye, except that both her mother and yers have insisted. Is there something I should ken?"

Tavish groaned. "They seem intent on making a match between us. They needn't bother. Yvaine will never accept me."

"Nay? Why is that?"

"She thinks I'm the cause of the problems she's encountered, not the one trying to save her from them. She all but accused me of being involved in a conspiracy against her da."

Toran frowned. "That's daft. None of our clan attacked him."

"But we still dinna ken who did. Or who attacked his

daughter. I did manage to do some damage, even if I failed to stop him."

"We still dinna ken who's behind this, damn it. We've learned naught. I've placed some men in the camp with the friendlier lairds' contingents. Donal has men there, too, of course. We're keeping an eye on developments. But given the number of strangers in our glen, it might have been someone who snuck in and left immediately after the attempt failed."

"Like Kilgore? I think ye are right about at least part of that. The name he gave Yvaine has to be a lie." His gaze roved over the great hall as groups made their way out to the bailey or up the stairs. Tavish turned in time to see Donal MacNabb shepherd his wife and daughter up the stairs, one of Bhaltair's men a few paces behind them.

"Niall and Ailbeart will alternate standing guard in the hall outside their chambers, with others of Bhaltair's men taking their place as needed," Toran told him. "If Yvaine decides she must leave her chamber, she'll be escorted, even to the privy. So will her parents. There have been two attacks on members of that family. I willna tolerate any more. Men will be on watch down here during the night as well."

"Then what do ye want me to do?" It seemed his father had the situation well in hand.

"I want ye to do as yer mothers have requested and stay near Yvaine, as soon as ye return from the hunt tomorrow. She'll be focused on ye—"

"Irritated by me, ye mean," Tavish interrupted.

Toran grinned. "She willna notice Bhaltair's other men following her and keeping watch on anyone near her."

"What about Donal? Surely he willna accept a guard."

"My cousin Jamie and he go back as far as Jamie and I do. The three of us will stick close together during the hunt and anywhere outside of the meetings in my solar." Toran inclined his head toward a tall man just standing up on the far side of the great hall. "Jamie arrived late from Fletcher. I had begun to fear he would not arrive at all."

"It must seem strange, having the three of ye back together in the same place."

Toran smiled as his cousin waved and started toward them. "Nay, not strange at all."

13

The noise of men and horses filling the bailey woke Yvaine the next morning. At first, she worried that there was trouble. She knelt on the window seat and studied the crowd below her. Ah, of course, the grand hunt. There was her father with the Lathan laird and another man she didn't recognize, but who had that Lathan look about him. Tall, well-muscled, and auburn-haired. With them were the big head guard she'd seen often the past few days, and others she supposed were his men.

Then she spotted Drummond and Tavish approaching them. From this distance, the brothers were nearly indistinguishable from each other. Nearly, but not entirely. Drummond, two years older, was slightly more muscular and carried himself with the assured air of command that a well-respected heir might develop.

However, Tavish, slightly taller and leaner, was the one who captured her interest. There was an air of watchfulness about him. His gaze, like the Lathan guards', never stopped scanning the crowd. He expected trouble but didn't know from where.

Why did their visions have to be so damned unreliable?

Suddenly, the idea of the hunt seemed desperately dangerous. She knew how these hunts worked. Men would scatter into
the surrounding countryside, searching for deer and smaller
game for the Aerie's tables. She'd heard there would be a feast
at the end of the gathering, so success today was necessary and
men would stay out until they had game to bring back. But so
many men armed and firing arrows at anything that moved?
She shuddered, then recalled that not only would the men in
the bailey be going. Likely many of the men camped in the glen
would also join them. Including, possibly, her attacker. Or her
father's, if indeed they were two different men.

Her only solace was that she had not dreamt of any disas-
ters associated with the hunt. Had her mother? She dressed
quickly, unbolted and opened her door to cross the hall, but
stopped short when she spotted a strange man standing near
her parents' doorway.

He gave her a reassuring smile. "Lady Yvaine. I am Ailbeart,
one of the men Laird Lathan assigned after yer father
requested ye be guarded. I'll be yer escort today."

"Not Tavish?" The words were out before she thought them.
Not Tavish? Of course not. She'd just seen him in the bailey,
preparing to join the hunt. Why would she care whether he
escorted her or someone else did the duty? She didn't need an
escort, and she certainly didn't want Tavish to do it. Did she?

She didn't know this Ailbeart. He could be lying to her. The
thought flashed through her mind to step back, slam her door
and lock it, but it quickly fled. He seemed trustworthy. And he
seemed bigger than the man who had attacked her. That gave
her some confidence that she would be well served to accept
his help.

"Is my mother up?"

"I heard some movement a short time ago, Lady Yvaine. I
imagine the noise in the bailey woke her, as I suspect it
woke ye."

"It did." Gathering her courage, Yvaine crossed the hall and knocked on her mother's door. She kept their guard visible in the corner of her eye. He was too close for her comfort and if he made any move, she would do her best to escape him. But he stayed still as a statue while she waited for her mother to answer the door.

In moments, she did. "Ah, daughter. I see ye have met Ailbeart."

"Ye kenned he would be here?"

"Aye. And I approve." She beckoned Yvaine inside and, after thanking their guard, closed the door behind her. "Can ye see the preparations for the hunt from yer window? Did ye see yer da?"

"Aye. With the Lathan laird, another man, and several guards. Also, with Drummond and Tavish."

"So, everyone is going."

"Not everyone," Yvaine answered, glancing back toward the door, meaning the guard left behind to watch over them. "I came to ask if ye had any visions concerning the hunt."

"Nay. Did ye?"

"Naught. I hope that bodes well. I dinna like the risk Da is taking."

"Yer da thrives on risk. *Dinna fash*. I am not. There is no one more capable than yer da."

"Then explain the knife in his shoulder," Yvaine groused.

"I canna. But he wasna badly hurt and Aileana took care of him. I worry less for him here than I do at home."

Yvaine didn't see how that could be. At home, they weren't surrounded by strangers. "How long will they be gone?"

Ellie shrugged. "It depends on how soon they are success-ful. It could be a few hours or all day. If they are not successful, I would expect the lairds to return and leave their men to continue the hunt into the night."

Which might mean Tavish would not return until very late,

or not until tomorrow. Something twisted deep in Yvaine's belly. As much as he irritated her, she didn't like the thought of him at risk, either.

Tavish rode out of the bailey at Drummond's side. The brothers would hunt together, escorted by three more of Bhaltair's best men. Their father would hunt with his old friends, Donal and Jamie, plus Bhaltair, and three more men. But the two groups would stay close together. The other participating lairds rode with their own guards and one Lathan as a guide. One laird, old MacBean, opted to stay behind with his men.

Tavish didn't like the idea of a stranger left inside the Aerie while the laird, his heir and he were outside of it, but there were plenty of Lathan warriors still in place to guard the keep, the MacKyrie women, and to keep the strangers under control and out of areas where visitors didn't belong.

The day had dawned clear and cold. It made for brisk riding as they headed out through the glen and into the forest beyond it. Men from the tent camp joined up with their lairds and continued on, following the directions of their Lathan guides. Each group headed out at an angle from its neighbors. Tavish hoped that would ensure enough separation between the hunting parties to prevent unfortunate accidents.

Or deliberate murder.

He glanced at Donal. The man rode easily, as if unconcerned by any possible threat. He'd survived much in his years at Lathan, and more since moving to MacKyrie. Perhaps he was more accepting of anything life—or death—threw his way. But Tavish was not.

The attacks on Donal and Yvaine still weighed on him. And on all of the Lathans. At least his latest vision and the attack on Yvaine had spurred them into taking action to guard all of the

MacKyries. But what would her attacker do next? And was he with a hunting party or had he stayed with the laird left behind in the Aerie? Or had he left the area once his planned attacks failed?

Tavish didn't hope for the latter. His sleep last night had been dreamless, but he would be a fool to discount the possibility of more danger. He had full confidence in the men left in the keep to guard Yvaine and her mother or he wouldn't be here now. Toran wanted both his sons in attendance, but Tavish would have stayed behind, no matter how it might look to the assembled lairds, if he had any doubts about Yvaine's safety while they were away.

As they headed into the trees, the morning became darker, more still and shadowed. Their small group moved quietly; the horses well trained to make as little noise as possible. They didn't expect to encounter the game they sought this close to the keep, but Tavish hoped they would soon. He didn't like the feeling that came over him as soon as they got under the trees. Not a vision, but more like the sense of foreboding that had plagued him before the MacKyrie party's arrival at the Aerie, only stronger.

"Be vigilant," he warned softly. "I sense something."

"What?" Drummond, closest to him, asked the question the others must be thinking.

"I dinna ken. Just be prepared for anything."

Toran frowned and exchanged a glance with Donal and Jamie. "Put Donal in the center. Guards at all corners. The rest of us around him. Now."

"Nay," Donal objected, but Toran silenced him with a look, and the rest positioned themselves as Toran directed. Satisfied that they had covered the angles as well as they could, they continued on. They avoided narrow trails that would force them to proceed single file. Instead, they kept to more open clearings and glens as much as possible, pausing often to listen and look, both for the game that was their quarry and for other hunters.

Toran's cousin Jamie was the first to spot the big buck on the far side of a clearing they approached. He raised a hand and closed his fist, halting them, then pointed. Toran nodded for him to take the shot, but he shook his head. "Donal's got a better angle," he said softly. "There's a tree in my way."

Without comment, Donal nocked an arrow and let fly. He hit the target, but it wasn't a killing shot. The buck lurched forward far enough to clear Jamie's obstruction. His arrow hit the mark and brought down the deer.

"Well done, both of ye. We'll be sitting in front of the hearth fire early this day," Toran said and started forward. An arrow whistled out of the trees on Tavish's side. Before he could move or shout a warning, it embedded itself in Donal's good arm.

"Not again," Donal groused as he slid to the ground behind his horse. He landed on his feet and crouched. Tavish and the others did the same, searching the woods for the marksman. Nothing moved.

"Who is after ye?" Toran's tone was aggrieved. "Ye didna cause this much trouble when ye lived here."

"I wish I kenned, but I dinna," Donal answered, then hissed as Jamie cut off the arrow's shaft and bound Donal's arm to hold the remainder in place and stop the bleeding.

"Anybody see anything yet?"After hushed negative responses to his question,Jamie muttered, "Aileana is going to be glad when ye leave."

"*Me?*" Donal gave Jamie an aggrieved glare."At least this arrow is only in my arm, not in my chest, like yers was. After what ye put her through all those years ago, she must still run, quaking in fear, anytime ye appear."

"Wheesht, both of ye," Toran commanded in a hiss. "We're not out of this yet."

Bhaltair slipped silently from tree to tree in the direction the arrow came from. After a few minutes, his whistle alerted them that whoever had tried to kill Donal again had fled the area.

He walked back to them without taking cover.

They stood and waited for him to reach them.

"Naught?" Toran's disappointment was evident in his voice.

"Gone. I found the spot he used. Crushed ground cover where he waited for his shot. He must have paralleled our path from the time we entered the woods until we stopped moving long enough to take down that stag. He's gone now."

"Or he found himself another place to lie in wait," Drummond observed.

Tavish shook his head. "I dinna think so. That feeling I had is gone."

Toran huffed out a breath, then pointed at two of the guards. "Collect that stag, then follow us. Cook will have to clean it. The rest of us will head back so Aileana can take care of Donal. Again."

———————

Yvaine and Ellie were in the great hall when Donal walked in, supported by Toran on one side and Jamie on the other. Ellie shot to her feet. "Not again!"

Yvaine's back had been to the door. At her mother's exclamation, she twisted around, then threw her legs over the bench and stood. "Da?"

"I'm fine. Aileana will have this healed in moments."

One of the guards who came in behind them ran for the herbal. Aileana appeared moments later and shook her head. "Donal! Ye are far more trouble than ye are worth."

"And always have been, milady," he teased. But his face had lost its usual color and sweat beaded his brow.

"Get him into my herbal, now," she said, and gestured in that direction. "On the table and off his feet."

Yvaine started to follow, but Ellie grabbed her arm. "Let her work without interference. If she needs something, she'll send for it. She'll tell us when she's done."

"But..."

"Nay, Yvaine. Yer da will get the best care possible."

Yvaine dropped onto the bench and covered her face with her hands. "Why does this keep happening? I've had nay vision that would warn of it."

"Nor have I, daughter," Ellie said, moving close and gripping her shoulder. "But yer father is tough, and has many friends here, who have kept him alive 'till now. Whether we can warn of trouble or not, they will continue to do so."

"'Tis not enough." Yvaine knew her words came out as a wail, but she couldn't help herself. She felt powerless. Frustrated. Ready to hit something or someone.

She looked up in time to see Drummond and Tavish Lathan enter the great hall. "Ach, just who I need to deal with right now."

"Daughter," Ellie said, her voice full of warning. "Behave. Those men helped save yer father. They dinna deserve yer anger."

"Everywhere Tavish goes, trouble follows for MacKyrie."

"Everywhere Tavish goes, he goes to keep MacKyries safe. He is not the source of the trouble."

"He seems so to me."

"And how do ye think ye seem to him?"

Yvaine didn't have an answer for that. And she didn't have time to come up with one. Drummond and Tavish approached. "Laird MacKyrie, Lady Yvaine," Drummond greeted them. "Donal was hit by an arrow. In his other arm, this time. Mother will see it removed and the damage repaired. He might have lost more blood on the way back, but Jamie bound up the wound. Please *dinna fash*. Donal will be well very soon."

"Whose arrow? I saw the lot of ye in the bailey before ye left. Such a great lot of ye couldna keep him safe?" Yvaine turned her gaze to Tavish and narrowed her eyes.

"It came from the trees beside us," Tavish said, not rising to her bait. "Bhaltair searched and found where the archer waited. He was gone."

"Excuse me," Drummond said then. "I must tell Cook there will soon be a buck waiting for her outside the kitchen. As ye might imagine, we didna take the time to dress it, but brought it, whole, back with us."

"Too bad ye didna bring my father back the same way," Yvaine muttered.

Ellie grabbed her hand and squeezed it. Hard. "Ye must forgive my daughter. She is upset about her father."

"Of course, she is," Tavish said in the same tone of voice Yvaine had used.

"Excuse us," Drummond repeated, grabbed Tavish's arm and pulled him away.

Ellie heaved an exasperated breath and collapsed onto the bench, frowning at her daughter. "What am I to do with ye? Either ye or yer da? Or any of ye, including those Lathan lads?"

"Take us home," Yvaine said. "Where we'll be safe."

"We might be," Ellie said wistfully, then she straightened. "'Tis possible. But 'tis not likely, not until we find out who is behind this. We could be ambushed on the way, and Aileana would not be there to help. Then someone *would* die. Nay, here we stay until this is solved." When her mother used her laird voice, Yvaine knew it was fruitless to argue.

She sank down beside her on the bench. "Wonderful."

14

O nce all the hunting parties had returned and turned their spoils over to the kitchen to prepare the next evening's feast, Toran called a council of war and demanded all the lairds attend without their retainers.

"Someone among ye has tried twice to kill Donal MacN-abb," he said as the door to his solar was closed behind the last laird to enter. He stood as the lairds erupted into a rumble of denials, leaned forward and planted his fists on his desk. He pinned them all with the glare Tavish knew all too well, a sign of his father at the end of his patience. "Worse, someone from among ye attacked his daughter. Perhaps the same person, perhaps not. Fortunately, she wasna badly harmed." His glare swept the room. "I want answers and I want them now. Who is behind this? And why?"

Tavish swept the chamber with his gaze. Most of the lairds looked angry and confused. Ellie MacKyrie remained calm even as the other lairds in the room turned to her. "Yer husband and daughter, Laird MacKyrie?" One of the lairds Tavish had met for the first time at this gathering looked at her with concern. "Have ye trouble at home that might have followed ye here?"

"None, Laird MacGregor," she answered calmly. "This began here. And it must end here."

"Well said, Laird MacKyrie," Toran told her. "It must end here. I want the names and clan affiliation of every person ye brought with ye, particularly anyone new to yer clan or to yer service." He held up a placating hand. "I dinna believe the attempted assassin is in this chamber. None of ye were in the glen the day Donal was stabbed with a dirk." Then his expression darkened, his brow lowering. "But ye were in the keep when his daughter was attacked, and all but one of ye were on the hunt with yer men. All armed with bows and arrows."

He let them react, denials filling the air, then held up a hand for silence.

"Earlier today, a coward shot at Donal from the trees in a surprise attack. Then he ran when his attempt failed to kill his target. The man who was my former arms master and who is now Laird MacKyrie's husband and arms master. A man who means much to both our clans." Toran paused to let that sink in, then continued. "Ye must be mindful of anyone trying to join your men—or to steal their weapons.Do ye ken anyone who might have a history with Donal MacNabb or the MacNabb clan? Or the MacKyries?"

"Or any connections to clan MacDuff?" Ellie spoke up, surprising Tavish. The crease between her brows indicated she might have surprised herself, as well. He expected her to let Toran continue with his demands, but it seemed the thought she'd just expressed had arisen in her mind unbidden and unexpected.

Toran's cousin, Jamie Lathan, there for Clan Fletcher, stood. "I hadn't thought of that, Ellie, but 'tis an interesting idea."

"MacDuff?" One of the lairds asked. "Why?"

"Donal was forced to kill the former MacDuff laird. He

coveted our glen and whisky more than me, but he attempted to force me into marriage in order to take control of them and my people, whom he would have enslaved in his mines. As he had done with his many previous wives, he would have cut short my life. Instead, Donal saved me and dealt MacDuff the justice he deserved."

"Why have we never heard this tale?" Another laird asked, his question echoed by others in a growing murmur.

"'Twas MacKyrie business. And it left Clan MacDuff under my hand." She turned to Toran. "What would ye have us do, Laird Lathan?"

MacDuff. That was the clan Kilgore was a sept of. Now it made sense. Tavish opened his mouth to speak, but his father shook his head, so he waited. Perhaps his father had already made the connection, but if he had, was Kilgore in custody?

"Tavish will collect yer information," Toran said, regaining control of the meeting. "Jamie, if ye would, assist Tavish. All of ye, see him before ye leave this chamber. Laird MacKyrie, not ye. Go see how yer husband fares."

She nodded and rose. "Thank ye, Laird Lathan."

Once she left, Toran stood and gestured for Tavish to take his place at the desk. Parchment, ink and quills were at the ready. For the next hour and more, Tavish thought of nothing save recording the information his laird demanded. Jamie sat by him and questioned the lairds about their people.

Toran remained by the door, Drummond at his shoulder, refusing all requests for exit, no matter the reason. One of the lairds muttered about being treated with disrespect, but returned to his seat when Toran gestured him away from the door with an open, upturned hand. However, his comment elicited more dissent.

"Ye canna keep us in here," MacBean complained and took a breath as if readying himself to continue, but the MacAnalen laird answered him before he could, and before Toran could intervene, saying, "I want the traitor found as soon as possible so we can all go home with our names cleared of any complicity in this."

A chorus of "ayes" quieted the discontented laird, and he sat back with arms crossed over his abundant belly.

Tavish felt sure MacBean was simply biding his time until the next opportunity to disagree about something the Lathan laird directed them to do. When Laird MacBean approached to provide the names of his men, Tavish met his gaze. "Do ye ken a man named Iver Kilgore?"

"Nay, I dinna. Why do ye ask?"

"Because he has tried to appear as though he came with ye and yer men."

MacBean straightened, his face going florid under a frown. "How dare he? And if ye suspect him, why put us through this?"

Toran stepped forward and raised his voice. "Because my son's comment should remind ye that ye all must be mindful of anyone trying to join yer men. Or of any missing weapons."

"Like the man ye detained for his lack of a dirk when MacNabb was stabbed in the glen?"

"Aye, exactly like that. That man was cleared, but someone has his dirk. And perhaps other weapons taken from some of yer men, as well."

MacBean's frown deepened. He provided his men's names, then returned to his seat.

Tavish knew keeping the lairds here was his father's way of impressing upon them that he was utterly serious about discovering who was behind all of this trouble. Tavish hoped in doing so, he didn't put at risk the treaty that he had worked more than twenty long years to achieve and maintain.

WHEN IT WAS FINALLY DONE AND THE LAST LAIRD LEFT THE solar, Tavish sat back and flexed his hand. He hadn't written so much, so steadily, since he'd been under the instruction of his tutor. Jamie picked up the stack of parchments, one for each laird's men, and scanned through them, then looked up at Toran. "If he's here, 'tis not obvious. These men are strangers to us, and only a little better kenned since their arrival, but their lairds didna seem hesitant about any of them."

"I didna think they would identify anyone so easily. I apologize for putting ye through that," he said to Tavish. "I wanted to force each laird to think about his men as suspects. One or more might have reacted in a way that would help us." His lips flattened into a resigned line. "None did. But they will have this on their minds for the rest of their stay, and they may notice aught that they would have missed before."

"That's it, then," Tavish announced. "MacBean doesna claim Kilgore. And Kilgore is a MacDuff sept. Laird MacKyrie was right to bring it up." It made sense. "I didna recall that connection until Ellie mentioned MacDuff. He probably came alone, taking advantage of the numbers of strangers here to blend in. We've seen him. We ken who he is. Now we need to find him."

"We will continue to search for him," Toran vowed, "but no one has seen him the last few days, unless he attacked Yvaine. Bhaltair kens his face. If he is still in the area, he canna hide for long."

"What if 'tis more than one person?"

Jamie's question made Tavish's belly ache. Could a MacDuff be after Donal and a different someone, the man Tavish had fought, want to harm Yvaine? Or had he misinterpreted his vision entirely? Was seeing Yvaine's death meant only to symbolize her father's?

"That is a worrisome notion." Toran frowned, glanced at Jamie, who shrugged, then back to Tavish.

"I dinna think 'tis true," Tavish answered. "More likely, someone wants to hurt Donal through Yvaine, or even Ellie. The Seer has been behind closed doors. Even if he wished to, he hasna had much chance to get to her."

"Donal would be devastated by harm befalling Yvaine," Jamie said. "If they canna get to him directly, she's the next best target. Or perhaps an even better one, because he would be forced to live with the knowledge that something in his past led to her death."

"The same could be said for her mother," Drummond added.

A wave if despair washed over Tavish. "I think ye may be right. We need to double the guard on Yvaine and her mother. Someone needs to be in the chamber with Yvaine."

"Who? How many lasses do we have who can fight well enough to protect her if someone breaks in?"

"I'll do it," Tavish said, then wished he'd kept his thoughts to himself when Drummond burst out laughing.

"'Tis not proper," Drummond said when he got control of himself. "And Donal will kill ye."

"I stopped one attack against her. I think he understands I want to keep her from harm, not take advantage of her."

"Nay, Tavish, Drummond is right," their father said. "But I will post more guards on the stairs and all along that hallway. No one will go there without my or Donal's permission. Even ye," he added with a tight smile.

Tavish should have felt relieved to have been spared this duty. Yvaine would not have accepted his presence with anything approaching good grace. But he was disappointed. He had made himself responsible for her, yet his family kept pulling him away to deal with the gathering. The other lairds. The hunt. He hadn't seen Yvaine all day save when they brought Donal in. She'd rounded on him then. Would she ever learn to greet him as a friend? To trust him? To accept that he cared for her?

He wasn't optimistic.

ON HER FATHER'S ORDERS, YVAINE WOULD SPEND THE NIGHT IN her mother's chamber. The healer had confined him to a cot in her herbal where she could keep an eye on him, and where guards could block access to the chamber and the hallway leading to it and to the kitchen from the great hall.

A knock on the door startled Yvaine into standing.

"Who is it?"

Ellie's voice remained calm, so Yvaine took a breath and resumed her seat.

"'Tis Cook, Laird MacKyrie," the guard Niall told them. "With yer supper."

"Thank ye. Please come in."

The door swung open to the portly cook, their guard's greater size framing her from behind. She stepped in, and before she could attempt to curtsey with a full tray in her hands, Yvaine jumped up and said, "Thank ye, Cook. Let me help ye with that." She took the tray and set it on the nearby table.

"Ye will send for me if ye need aught else, aye?" The woman glanced from Yvaine to Ellie and back again.

"What news?" Ellie asked. "We've heard naught since midday."

Cook wrung her hands. "Ach, everyone in the keep is on edge, waiting for the next attempt on someone's life. I'm the only person the guards will allow into this chamber, saving yer husband, Laird MacKyrie."

"Call me Ellie, Cook, please."

The woman smiled and continued, "The only person I trust with yer food is myself. I will take good care of ye."

Ellie stood and took her hand. "Thank ye. Yer care means a great deal to us."

"Now, dinna let that get cold. I'll leave ye to yer supper, but send one of the lads if ye need aught else." She moved to the door, bobbed her head, then exited.

Niall gave the cook a smile as he closed the door, blocking them from Yvaine's view.

"Let's eat, shall we?" Her mother's invitation brought her attention back to the tray and the scents wafting from it. Her stomach growled.

Once they were seated, Ellie remarked that she had expected Tavish would be among their guards, but she hadn't seen him. "Ye owe him an apology, daughter, for the way ye spoke to him this afternoon."

Yvaine regretted her words, spoken in the heat of the moment, and in the shock and dismay that her father had been attacked again, but she hated to admit it. "Perhaps he understands we are well guarded and he is not needed."

"Ye ken none of this was Tavish's fault," her mother continued.

Yvaine hated to admit that, too. He tried to keep her safe and all she did was fight with him, insult him and threaten him.

"He didn't deserve yer accusations, daughter."

"I canna apologize to him if he isna here."

"Perhaps he'll come by later," Ellie remarked, then went back to eating, seeming to drop the subject.

Yvaine was not fooled. Her mother disapproved of the way she had treated Tavish, and disagreed with her suspicions about him. But until her visions returned, they would not know anything for certain.

The tension was wearing on Ellie. Yvaine could see it in her posture, the dark circles forming under her eyes, and the lines bracketing her mouth. She'd come here to be helped by the healer and just as she began to feel better, fear for her family made her worsen. It wasn't fair. None of this was fair, Yvaine thought, least of all that she was a lass, and was not allowed to help find the person behind these attacks on her da. Or the man who had attacked her. Tavish had saved her that day, and had said he was prepared to do it again. But his visions, like hers, failed to provide enough information for either of them to act. They seemed to learn just enough to concern them and make every move, every thought, every plan, about survival. This was no way to live.

She had to do something. But what? She had only one strength, one ability, to use toward solving the problem, and she was weak. But what if she merged her talent with her mother's? Even with Tavish's. There were three seers here, without an informative vision among them. But what if they worked together somehow?

"Mother, is it possible for seers to merge their talents? To share a vision and make it sharper, clearer, more complete?"

"What an interesting notion," Ellie exclaimed as she moved to her chair by the hearth to relax with some needlework, something she rarely did. "How do ye think that would work?"

"I dinna ken. But if ye, Tavish and I could somehow instruct ourselves to have the same dream, the same vision, would it help us to see more? Would we need to be together? Or even touching? Or what if someone like Aileana or Eilidh could form a...I dinna ken...a bridge between us. If we would see each other's visions, each of us might add to what we finally saw. To reveal the entire vision, not just a small piece of it."

Ellie set aside her needlework and sat, eyes closed and silent. Anyone who did not know her might think she had fallen asleep, but Yvaine knew this was her mother in deep thought. Finally, she opened her eyes. "I dinna ken if it will work, but we must try it. Here? Nay, in the herbal. We'll join

Aileana there. She can send for her twins and we will see what we will see."

She stood and smiled. "Ye have given me hope, Daughter. Thank ye."

"Ye are most welcome, Mother, but I dinna ken if this will work. It may come to naught."

"Or it may reveal all we need to ken. Come."

She crossed to the door, opened it and peered out. "Something is wrong."

15

Tavish set aside his ale and turned his attention inward, ignoring for the moment the story Drummond was telling his son Rory as they sat by the hearth in the great hall. The evening meal was long over and most of the servants had retired for the night. Drummond would go soon. He was responsible for getting Rory to settle down and go to bed before Morven came looking for them. Though Tavish would also enjoy seeing his eldest brother bow to his wife, he couldn't give them his attention at the moment.

That feeling was back. The one Tavish hated. The one that told him something was wrong, but didn't tell him what, or where or for whom. Except he knew the last. Yvaine and her father.

"Look Da," Tavish heard Rory say as if from a very great distance. "Tavish is doing that thing again. Going away."

"Then let us go away, too. 'Tis getting late, and time I got ye upstairs to bid yer mother goodnight."

Tavish remained dimly aware of them leaving him alone by the hearth. The solitude helped as he sought the source of his disquiet. It felt...up. Yvaine's chamber? That didn't seem right.

He stood and, with the help of the handrail, made his way safely up the stairs despite the thrall he held himself in, fighting to get a better sense of the danger.

Something was wrong. There were no guards in the hall. Yvaine's door was open and her room was empty. Where was she? If only he had some of Drummond's ability to find people and things.

At that moment, the door to Donal and Ellie's chamber across the hall opened. Ellie peered out and frowned. "Something is wrong," he heard her say, then she noticed him. "Tavish. Where is everyone?"

He shook his head. "Where is Yvaine?"

"With me."

"Close yer door and lock it. Bar it. Close and lock yer shutters. I will see— "

He felt more than heard someone behind him. As he turned, he pulled his dirk.

"Tavish, 'tis I."

"Bhaltair. Where are yer men?"

"Downstairs. Searching. Niall came downstairs to me and said he overheard someone say Yvaine had been seen outside. Ye ken how voices can carry in this place. He thought she'd gotten by him while he talked to Cook after she delivered their supper."

"She's with Ellie." He could see relief written in the drop of Bhaltair's shoulders and the gentle shake of his head.

"I came up to replace Niall at Laird MacKyrie's door. The others are out looking for Yvaine. I'll speak to them, then go tell the others they can stop the search."

Bhaltair went to the door and knocked. "Laird MacKyrie, 'tis Bhaltair and Tavish."

Tavish heard the sounds of things moving and the door opened. "Take us to the herbal," Ellie said without preamble. Yvaine has an idea. We need ye, too, Tavish. And Eilidh."

"Follow me," Bhaltair told her. Ellie turned back to the open doorway and waved Yvaine out.

"Tavish. Ye are here. I want to apologize…"

"That can wait. Let's get ye safe," he told her and gestured for her to follow her mother. He brought up the rear and kept watch behind as they went, expecting someone to appear out of an open doorway or chase them down the hall. No one did.

He realized his sense of unease had faded. They were moving, doing something positive to solve their problem. To save themselves. Was that the answer? That his sense of doom came on when nothing was being done to alter or eliminate a danger? Still, he wondered, who had Niall overheard?

At the bottom of the stairs, several guards surrounded them and went with them to the herbal. Once they were inside, Bhaltair sent Niall to fetch Eilidh and another to call off the search for Yvaine. Aileana was already there, asleep on the floor, but she woke when they all came in. Donal remained unconscious. "Healing sleep," Aileana told Ellie. "He's fine."

Ellie nodded. "Thank ye. Yvaine had an idea, but we need ye and the twins, or we think we do."

Eilidh arrived then and, with a nod to Bhaltair, entered the herbal. While Bhaltair deployed his men to guard the approach to the herbal and to assign more men outside, Yvaine described her idea.

"'Twould be something akin to what ye did between me and Tavish," Ellie explained to Aileana. But with three of us, we thought it might work if Eilidh could help join us all together."

"Laird MacKyrie," Tavish said.

"Ellie," she corrected him.

"Ellie, ye ken what I saw the last time. Do ye think 'tis wise for Yvaine…"

"She can handle it. 'Tis only a vision, one we seek to make sure doesna come to pass."

"I dinna wish to harm her."

"I ken it," Yvaine said. "Whatever it is, I ken ye will take care of me."

Tavish's heart swelled. He'd been waiting to hear those words. Yvaine had finally accepted him. Perhaps the next steps would be easier. He wanted to make her his. He'd convinced her of this much. Surely the rest could follow. He nodded, too fraught to give her the smile that was beaming from his heart, warming his insides and stinging his eyes, even as the prospect of what they proposed to do chilled his blood.

They had something new to try. But if it worked, Yvaine might see her death.

"I must speak to Bhaltair," Aileana said. "We will be vulnerable while we do this. He must be aware." She left them and went out into the hall. Tavish heard her voice and Bhaltair's deep rumble, then she returned. "Very well. We can start when we are ready."

She held her hand out to Ellie, who reached for Yvaine. Tavish took Yvaine's other hand, fighting to control the longing that her touch evoked, and his sister's, who joined with their mother. "We canna be between ye. We'd need another healer and my son Jamie is far away, at Keith with his bride. So, we will try this with Eilidh and I together, facing ye, all connected. Let's sit."

They settled on the floor and got comfortable.

"Drummond is here," Tavish suddenly recalled. "His talent is not strong, but it might be enough."

"Let's try this first," Yvaine said.

"I agree," Aileana replied. "Drummond is with his family for the night. But I will send for him if we need him."

"Very well," Ellie said. "Close yer eyes. Empty yer minds of all save my voice. Breathe slowly and deeply." She paused, then spoke more softly. "Listen to my voice. Silence surrounds us. Darkness fills us. But it is warm and comforting. And we are together." After another long pause, she murmured, "We can sense each other. Reach out to each other and let the visions come."

Tavish felt Yvaine and Eilidh's hands in his, but even more strangely, he felt both of them inside him. The MacKyrie Seer and his mother were there, too. Eilidh's presence was familiar, something he'd known since they shared a womb. His mother's, too, was warm, familiar, comforting and encouraging. The MacKyrie Seer brought a sense of power with her, leashed for the moment, but available. He gathered them together, then turned his attention to the one he wanted within him the most, even as he feared what this experience might do to her. Yvaine, seemed to reach out to him, to merge most fully with him, welcoming him, with no trace of animosity. He felt accepted. And ready.

There were flashes of...something...then Ellie said, "breathe deep, as if ye will sleep. Let the visions come."

Tavish was floating...following the lass. Yvaine. Watching her braid sway in time with the movement of her hips. Waiting for her to turn and smile at him as she always did. When it came, he smiled back. She saw him. Then she turned the corner and disappeared. He paused, fearing what he knew he would see next, but knowing he had to follow her. They all had to see. He rounded the corner of the kirk and halted, horror filling him, roiling his belly, despite his foreknowledge. He squeezed his eyes shut, then opened them again, hoping the vision would change. She was still there. On the ground, that gorgeous bronze hair wrapped around her long, graceful neck. Graceful no more, it bent at an unnatural angle, and her sightless eyes gazed up at him as if begging him to save her. Whoever had done it was gone.

He was too late. Again.

YVAINE SWALLOWED A SCREAM. THAT WASN'T HER ON THE
ground. It was only a dream. A vision. Tavish's vision. Not real.
Never real. She felt her mother's solid, confident presence next
to her. It would never happen. Tavish, holding her other hand
in his big, strong grip, would keep her safe. Why couldn't she
see anything that would tell her what to believe? She had
nothing to add. Nothing to share.

But it was his vision. Could it mean he wanted her dead?
Nay, that made no sense.

What had that lass on the ground seen in her last
moments? Had she seen the face of the man who'd done this to
her? She fought to relax. To let herself fall into that deep, dark,
warm place of dreams. Aileana met her gaze and nodded.
Somehow, that simple gesture calmed her. She closed her eyes,
and she was there.

*She would not be kept a prisoner in her chamber. She would
not be confined. She would go where she willed. She drifted here
and there, recognizing some things that showed themselves as if
through a thick mist, then receded again, like the smithy and the
weavers' looms, but long corridors, stretches of open ground, and
stone walls defied location. She kept going, glanced back and saw a
shadow pass over a bright spot on a floor. Someone followed her.
Watched her. But who? She turned to confront him. He was there.
This time, he didn't fade away. He approached. Did she know him?
She couldn't see him clearly. How could she tell the others when she
couldn't describe his face? While she fretted, he came closer. She
tried to move away from him, but somehow, he got behind her. He
picked up her braid and stroked its silky length.She was powerless
to stop him, unable to move away. Every time she turned her head
to try to see him, he drifted out of her view, behind her. Her heart
beat faster. Suddenly he wrapped her braid around her throat,
caressing her skin with her hair, his fingers never touching her. She
couldn't think. She could only turn her head, but every time she
did, he tightened the braid around her neck. Soon, she fought to*

breathe. She couldn't stop this from happening. She was going to die.

She woke up.

Tears streamed down Yvaine's cheeks as she became aware that she was still alive and gasping, but still able to breathe. With a cry, she dropped the hands she gripped and turned into Tavish's open arms. She was shocked to realize he was just what and who she needed. Strong, warm, caring, smart, and a Seer like her. A man who understood what she was going through, because it was his talent—and his curse, too. How had this happened? She wanted to stay in the comfort and safety of his arms forever. But she couldn't. She could feel the others' concern for her and she fought to get her reaction under control. Tavish held her until she calmed enough to remember and to speak. Then she sat up, gave him a grateful smile, turned to the others and said, "I've seen the man before."

"Where?" Aileana's question erupted at the same time as Ellie's "When?"

"Two days ago. Or three? Let me think. In the great hall, perhaps. That must have been where." She choked and took a breath while Tavish rubbed her back in soothing circles. "He was the man in the vision. The man who means to kill me."

"Or yer da," Aileana said with a glance at Donal's sleeping form.

"Could he have help?" Eilidh's question landed like a rock dropped into a pool, causing ripples of consternation to spread outward until everyone's face wore the same frown and the same worried look in their eyes.

Tavish spoke up to fill the silence. "I never got a clear look at him, but perhaps I ken him, too. Kilgore. I think he's acting alone, else there wouldha been more attempts on both of ye by now. He's been going slowly, picking his target, time, and locations."

"Not well, thank God," Ellie remarked.

"Could that be on purpose?" Eilidh asked. "If he means to harm, but not to kill. To frighten us. The more he does, the harder it must be to get close to either of ye, to succeed, after he's made everyone more watchful."

"But why?" Tavish thought they'd come up with his motive after the meeting with the lairds, but they'd assumed he meant to kill, not simply to terrorize.

"To make us suffer," Yvaine answered. "Why else?"

"For what? And why now? Why here? Why not come into our glen and do this?" Glints of anger shone in Ellie's eyes.

"Because he wouldha been recognized there and stopped? Here, he's with people who dinna ken him?"

"To blend in," Ellie said.

Tavish ran a hand through his hair. "Da had the lairds list all their men, to make them think about who they brought, and who they were aligned with. No one said anything about having someone with them they were unsure of. Kilgore has to be the one and only."

"Perhaps they were embarrassed to admit bringing him."

"'Tis possible. We assumed he slipped into the glen and up to the Aerie with other lairds' men," Tavish told them. "But what if one of the lairds lied? What if one kens who this man is and why he's here? Why would he help him?"

"Perhaps he isna, but he's heard someone is impersonating one of his men," Eilidh continued. "What if he is attempting to deal with the problem himself? Especially after what Toran had them do, he'd have to ken the danger will be associated with him, even if it didna come with him."

"Or he prefers to ignore it until after they leave here," Tavish added.

"What if the man comes in during the feast?" Yvaine asked. "Everyone will be inside the keep."

"MacKyries will be guarded," Tavish declared to Ellie. "I

dinna see how else ye can be part of the celebration, save to keep others away from ye."

"As far as the reach of a thrown dirk or an arrow?" Yvaine shook her head. "Ye canna guard against everything."

"Only by doing as yer da threatened," Ellie remarked, "And locking us all away in our chambers until the strangers leave."

Tavish shook his head. "All that does is delay the confrontation and make the problem harder. If they ken ye well enough to hold a grudge, they will ken where to find ye along yer way home. They could strike anywhere along the route. Nay, we need to find Kilgore and get a confession. And find out if anyone else is involved. Or ye willna be safe, even at MacKyrie."

———

TAVISH WAS PRETERNATURALLY AWARE OF YVAINE SITTING NEXT to him. Her warmth under his hand as he stroked her back and tried to soothe her had the opposite effect on him. Her rioting emotions made his control harder to maintain. He could smell her fear and anxiety, and he longed for the day he would detect the scent of her arousal as she lay in his arms.

But, today was not that day, even though she had turned into his arms as she came out of the vision of her death, seeking comfort she knew he would give her. By acknowledging his attempts to keep her safe, she'd made the first step closer to him. This was another. But tomorrow, they could be back to being at odds again. He dared not celebrate too soon.

Her attention was on her mother. Ellie's had shifted from their discussion to her sleeping husband. She watched him for a moment, then looked to Aileana. "When will he awaken?"

"In the morning," the healer told her. "Unless ye need him sooner. I can wake him now, or any time before he awakens naturally. He is healed. I only thought to keep him from opening his wound. The skin looks newly healed, but the muscle I knitted back together is still weak. It will remain vulnerable for another day while his body recuperates from losing so much blood."

"Thank ye, healer, I understand. Leave him to his rest. I was being daft and selfish, wanting the comfort of his embrace. I can wait." She summoned a small smile for the others around her. "We all need to rest. Let us sleep on what we have learned this evening, and perhaps, tomorrow, we will learn more."

She pushed to her feet and held a hand out for Yvaine. "Come, daughter. As yer da wishes, we will bide together tonight."

Tavish nearly reached for Yvaine's hand as she stood, but knew that would give away too much about how he felt about her. He stood up next to her, then helped his twin to her feet. They both assisted their mother from the floor.

"Go on," she bid them. "Get some sleep. I'll stay here with Donal so he doesn't wake disoriented in the night. There are guards aplenty all around the herbal. I'll be well. And Bhaltair will see ye two looked after," she added, smiling at Ellie and Yvaine. "Rest easy."

Tavish kissed her cheek, then followed Eilidh, Yvaine, and her mother out into the hall. Bhaltair awaited them and led them across the great hall, now empty and dark save for the remnants of the banked but still glowing hearth fire, then up the stairs. Eilidh left them at the top of the stairs to go to her chamber.

More guards were already posted in the hallway outside the MacKyrie chamber doors. "Rest well, Laird MacKyrie. Lady Yvaine," Bhaltair told them, opened their door, and gestured them inside.

"I'll be out here," Tavish said as Yvaine passed him.

"Tavish, nay. Surely ye need to rest, too. And these men will be here to keep us safe."

"Nonetheless, I will." Tavish said and gestured her into her mother's chambers. "Good night."

"Good night, Tavish," she replied. "Thank ye for all ye have done. I never truly apologized to ye. I am sorry."

"I ken it. Now get some sleep. Dreamless sleep, lass."

She nodded and stepped inside. He pulled the door closed, reminding her to lock it before it closed completely. He heard the bolt engage. Satisfied, he turned to Bhaltair. "I'm going to sleep across their doorway. Yer men can take up positions in the hall wherever ye deem will give them the best advantage."

"Aye, and on the stairs, as well. They'll rotate positions every half hour to help them stay alert, and I've assigned only men well-used to working together. There willna be a repeat of earlier, and nay strangers on this hall. Dinna fash if ye sense movement around ye. Only if it comes close."

Tavish snorted. If he had a vision, he wouldn't wake in time to save himself or anyone else. "If I understand what ye are implying, it willna matter if I sense someone coming close. It will be too late for me by then."

"And for them," Bhaltair added with a nod toward the guards coming up the stairs.

Of course. Tavish regretted his insensitive remark. No one would get to him without first going through Bhaltair's men. He nodded, his expression grim, then went across the hall and stripped the pallet and cover from the bed Yvaine had used. Those he put on the floor in front of the doorway where she and her mother would sleep, or try to. He stood next to it, eyeing Bhaltair's men. He knew all of them. Satisfied, he lay down.

That was a mistake. The bedding carried Yvaine's scent. He should have realized it would. Or perhaps on some subconscious level, he had, but didn't want to acknowledge that fact. Instead, he had gone for the one thing that would torment him, or perhaps bring him clearer visions through the night. Before he closed his eyes, one of the guards kindly removed the nearest torch to a sconce farther away. The hall was not absolutely dark, but dim enough to be restful. He could see why Bhaltair had his men shift positions so often. They would be in danger of drowsing without some purposeful movement.

He closed his eyes and did not dream.

16

Kilgore watched from the shadows beside the keep's north tower as smoke rose from the rear of the Aerie's stables. In moments, bright orange flames licked up one side and panicked shouts broke the stillness of the night. Thuds and screams of terrified horses trying to break out of their stalls added to the din.

Someone banged on a pot, or rang a bell. He couldn't see which it was, and didn't care. People poured out of the keep, some with buckets headed for the central well, while others ran for implements to use to pull down burning thatch and wood, and shovels to throw dirt and smother them. In moments, horses, some with their heads covered by blankets, followed stable lads out into the bailey away from the burning building. Others were led out by Lathan men who turned them over to the lads, then ran back to retrieve more. The horses still in their stalls screamed and butted against walls or stall doors, intent on escape. The noise they made added to the confusion.

Kilgore waited until the rush of people from the keep trailed off, then moved quickly with the same urgency as everyone else hurrying around the bailey. When he reached the keep's door, he entered and closed it behind him. The MacKyrie laird, MacNabb, and his daughter were in here, somewhere. With everyone outside, it should be a simple matter to locate them. They would be in the only chamber still guarded.

Silence reigned in the great hall. He studied his surroundings carefully, ensuring no one remained in it so he could mount the stairs unobserved, then he proceeded.

At the top, he heard voices. A torch burned low beyond a group of men standing outside a chamber door far down the darkened hall. Kilgore paused, watchful, until another clanging alert sounded outside and everyone's attention riveted through the open door of the chamber across the hall, one that looked into the bailey. He took advantage of the diversion and ducked around the corner into the crossing hallway, and waited. From the tone of the conversation, he could tell some of the Lathan guards had already answered the call to help fight the fire, and the ones left behind were eager to join them. They didn't worry him. They'd soon be gone. But the man who'd kept him from Donal MacNabb, Tavish Lathan, stood next to a pile of bedding in front of the MacKyrie door. He could identify him and connect him to MacNabb.

Kilgore estimated the distance to the Lathan. Even if the other guards left, without some distraction, Lathan would see him coming long before he could reach him. He could not take him by surprise.Would he leave, too?

He stayed where he was, pondering how to gain the advantage he sought. He hadn't created the diversion at the stables to be stymied by one man.

Then he heard footsteps ascending the stairs. He shrank back into the dark hallway as another man headed for the group outside the chamber door.

"Who are ye?"

The Lathan was alert. Kilgore would give him that. The new man hadn't taken two steps toward the guarded door before the Lathan challenged him.

"I'm a MacKyrie guard. We all saw the fire from the glen. Men from all the clans have come up to help fight the fire or save the horses. I came to make sure my laird is safe."

"She is," the Lathan answered. "And her daughter. They're both within."

Kilgore clenched a fist. Where was MacNabb?

"I'm Tavish Lathan." He knocked on the door and in moments, it opened. "Laird MacKyrie," he addressed the woman who answered, but never took his gaze off of the newcomer, "this man claims to be one of yer guards. Do ye ken him?"

"Aye, I do. What is happening?"

"A fire broke out in the stables. 'Tis—" The clang of more bells or beaten pots halted his words. "Damn, they're calling for more help."

"We'll go," one of the other remaining Lathan guards said. "Ye and this MacKyrie will be able to hold the door until we can return."

The daughter peered out the door and spoke to Tavish. "We canna stay here while everyone else is working to save the stable. I can help calm the horses."

"Out there?" The Lathan sounded incredulous. "Ye ken I willna allow it. I canna keep ye safe in that confusion. No one can."

Kilgore couldn't see her reaction, but her voice soon made her displeasure clear.

"Allow it?"

"Nor will I." Her mother's voice brooked no argument.

For a moment, Kilgore considered killing the MacKyrie laird as well, but he knew there was no point. The clan's leadership would simply go to her son. Better to leave her alive to suffer the loss of her husband. Or her daughter. Or both.

"Very well," she relented. "I'll help Cook. Everyone will be tired and hungry by the time they get the fire out."

The Lathan appeared to consider that idea, and nodded. "The kitchen will be crowded with people I trust. I'll escort ye, then join the firefighters. Laird MacKyrie, 'tis best if ye remain here, with yer guard. Yvaine will be safe in the kitchen. Cook wields a mighty cleaver."

The laird summoned a smile and nodded. "Ye two go do what ye can to help."

Kilgore waited until everyone descended the stairs. Some, the guards he presumed, exited the great hall, while at least two crossed it toward the kitchens. Once he heard a lone person cross the great hall and leave the keep, he slipped out of his hiding place and descended the stairs.

He hadn't dared remain in the woods to try again after his arrow missed MacNabb during the hunt. He'd expected to be able to confront him in his chamber after the diversion he created drew away his guards. But that damned MacKyrie guard had arrived. No matter. His quarry would be easier to kill in the confusion of the fire fight. No one had mentioned him. He must already be outside.

He knew MacNabb's luck wouldn't last forever. Kilgore would find him and finish him before the confusion of the fire died down. If he didn't, Kilgore knew where the daughter would be. No cook's cleaver would keep him from her if her father escaped him again.

He slipped out of the great hall into the firelit night.

———

Yvaine wiped her brow. She'd forgotten how hot a kitchen could get when the Cook wanted everything readied at once.

Venison stew bubbled in the huge iron pot in the main hearth while bread baked on either side. Initially, Cook had set her to slicing more vegetables for the pot. That done, she'd offered to prepare trays of bread and cheeses that Cook wanted placed on each table in the great hall, along with bowls of apples and pitchers of ale, cider, and water.

Some of the kitchen lasses carried cider and cups out to the men fighting the fire, and to the women on the line passing full buckets to the fire and empty ones back to the well. However, following Tavish's instructions, Cook would not let Yvaine out of her sight, so she stayed in the kitchen, and did whatever Cook wanted.

As much as she wanted to be useful, and though she'd suggested this, she wished she'd been able to help calm the horses. She worried that panicked horses would hurt themselves or each other. Or their handlers. And as Eilidh had told her, she had a way with animals. Eilidh had sensed right away something that Yvaine had long suspected.

"What's happening out there?" She asked one of the lasses returning with an empty pitcher.

"Ach, 'tis madness. The fire still rages, but they're keeping it confined to the stable, it seems."

"Did they get all the horses out?"

"Aye, I think so. A few were moved to the opposite side of the Bailey, but there's not enough space for them all. Most are being taken down to the glen, away from the smoke and the noise."

"That's good, then," Cook remarked and handed her a full pitcher. "Go on with ye, and have a care ye dinna get hurt."

"I'm careful," the lass declared, nodded, and left.

Yvaine watched her go.Cook must have seen her restlessness. No sooner had she glanced at the door out of the kitchen than Cook bustled up to set her a new task.

"Dinna be thinking it, lassie," Cook told her. "Ye will stay here, where I can keep an eye on ye. Our Tavish doesna want ye in danger, and there's muckle of that out in the bailey this night."

"I was just wishing I could help with the horses."

"Nay, ye ken ye canna. Mayhap later, when all is settled, and yer guards are not so busy."

Yvaine pursed her lips and nodded. Cook was right. Knowing what they did, she'd be foolish to put herself in more danger, and danger to her would compound danger to everyone around her. "Very well. What's next?" She wiped her hands on the apron Cook had given her when she arrived.

"Lady MacKyrie."

The male voice startled her. She turned to find the MacKyrie guard who'd taken over from the Lathans. And from Tavish. She spared a moment to hope Tavish was safe before she answered. "Aye?"

"Ye mother asks for ye, milady. If ye will come with me?" His gaze tracked to Cook, cleaver in hand, glaring suspiciously at him.

Yvaine frowned. "Is aught amiss?" Who was with her mother?

"I dinna ken, milady. She asked that I fetch ye."

"I'm sorry, Cook," Yvaine told her. "I should go see what she needs."

Cook set aside the cleaver and nodded. "Go on with ye, then, but dinna be thinking about setting foot outside this keep."

Yvaine gave her a grateful smile for her care. "I willna. Thank ye, Cook. If I can return to help ye, I will."

The guard walked her down the hall and across the empty great hall to the stairs.

She took the first step up when something hit the back of her head and everything went gray and spotted. "What..."

He snaked an arm around her and squeezed her ribs to hold her upright close against his side. She forced her head up, fighting to breathe. The pressure on her torso made her heart pound in panic. She panted and her knees buckled. He tightened his grip. Lifting her feet from the floor, he carried her upright to the door. She was conscious enough to try to twist out of his grip, but he held her tight. Then he hit her again, and everything went black.

HOURS PASSED IN MOMENTS, OR SO IT SEEMED TO TAVISH. HE looked up to see dawn beginning to light the eastern sky and realized they'd won. The fire was out. The horses were safe, and some of the stable structure had survived. People were heading into the keep to clean up, break their fast, and rest.

The stable was a mess. They would have to rebuild many of the stalls, walls and part of the roof, but with a few days' hard work, it would be as good as new. In the meantime, the horses could be kept in the bailey or hobbled down in the glen until the gathering was over and they could be moved into the secret stable in the tor's lower caverns.

He went to the well and found a bucket full of clear water someone had left behind. He picked it up and poured it over his head, relishing the cold, wet rush of it. Dropping the bucket, he scrubbed his soot-blackened hands on his wet shirt, then pushed his streaming hair out of his eyes and wiped his face on his sleeve. He wasn't clean, but he felt better.

He spotted his father and his father's cousin Jamie closer to the keep's door and headed their way. When he reached them, his father clapped him on the back. "Good work, son, and everyone. This could have been much worse."

"Do we ken how it started?" Tavish hadn't seen enough to be able to guess.

Toran's shoulders tensed. "We think someone set it delib-erately."

"Damn. Why would someone burn down a stable?"

"When we find out who did it, we'll get the answer to that question," Toran said, ignoring Tavish's first question. He wiped a hand across his forehead. "Let's go inside. I have a lot of people to thank."

They entered the great hall. Filled with Lathans and most of the visitors, except for the few who'd taken horses down to the glen, the noise of conversation, clinking cups and pitchers was deafening. Toran waited for a natural lull, then called out for silence. He held up a hand until he got everyone's attention.

"Lathan owes all of ye a debt of gratitude for yer work this night. Ye saved most of the stable, all of the horses, and kept the fire from wreaking more serious damage inside our walls. I'm especially grateful to the men of our visiting clans for fighting for this keep as ye would yer own. Now, go back to eating and drinking, then get some rest. Ye have earned it."

Amid the cheer that followed that pronouncement, Toran turned and headed for his solar. Jamie followed, but Tavish had another destination in mind. Yvaine was probably still in the kitchen. Judging by the amount of food and drink being consumed, the kitchen had been active all night, and Cook and her helpers were probably still hard at work.

The kitchen was indeed as chaotic as Tavish expected, but after a moment, he could see that it was organized chaos. Cook had everything under control, despite the fatigue that must be affecting all of them. But among all the lasses bustling here and there, he didn't see the one woman he wanted to find.

"Where is Yvaine?" Tavish mouthed his question when he managed to catch Cook's eye. She was across the chamber, but she understood him. She nodded and moved toward him, dodging her lasses who bustled about with trays of food headed for the great hall and others with pots or bowls of any number of things. He didn't try to follow it all. Instead, he kept his gaze on Cook. She reached him and frowned. "Are ye just coming in? 'Tis been a long night, aye?"

"It has. What have ye done with Yvaine?"

"Me? Naught. A guard came and fetched her. Said her mother wanted her."

Tavish tensed against the sinking feeling in his belly. "How long ago?"

"I dinna ken. An hour? More? I havena had the leisure to pay attention to the passing of time, not this night."

Tavish nodded, not wanting to upset her. "I understand. Thank ye. I will seek her upstairs."

Cook gave him a wink and a smirk at his black-smeared shirt. "Ye might want to clean up a wee before ye do."

He summoned a grin, turned and left her, only then letting the concern that hollowed his belly show on his face.

He threaded his way through the throng in the great hall and mounted the stairs two at a time. At the MacKyrie door, he knocked harder than was polite. Ellie called out, "Who is it?"

"'Tis Tavish, Laird MacKyrie. Is Yvaine with ye?"

The door opened and she gazed up at him with fright in her eyes. "Nay, not since she left with ye to help Cook."

"Have ye been asleep the whole time? Could she have returned?" He glanced over her robe-clad shoulder into the empty room.

"Nay, lad. She isna here. And now I am worried."

"I, too, but I will find her. I'll alert Bhaltair's men, too. Dinna go downstairs yet. The great hall is packed at the moment."

"Could she be there and ye just didna see her?"

"'Tis possible. I will look, never fear."

"Please..."

"I ken it. Now, keep ye safe in here. Lock the door until Donal or one of us Lathans ye ken comes for ye."

She nodded, stepped back and closed the door. Would she

do as he asked? Or like her daughter, would she head out as soon as she dressed, and risk herself to find her child? He hoped she had better sense.

Tavish headed back downstairs, that cold empty space in his belly growing with each step.

17

Yvaine came awake to a pounding headache and horror. The vision she'd seen last night when linked to Tavish and the others was coming true! And the guard standing over her was no guard. He was the man who intended to kill her.

He'd failed the first time.

He'd gotten to her again.

Why was she still alive? Was he waiting for her to wake up?

His back was to her, but she could see enough of his profile in the predawn glow to recognize him—or where they were. The sounds of the fire seemed distant, or blocked by the stone around them. Had he started the fire, or simply taken advantage of the diversion to get to her? Either way, it might be too late for her. She was in terrible trouble.

She suspected they were in the gap behind one of the crafters buildings and the keep's outer wall. Which meant there was no chance of anyone happening by. She had to think —or die.

The fire must be out. She didn't hear the crackle of burning wood and thatch, nor was a pall of smoke choking the bailey. She didn't hear the horses, or the shouts and other commotion that she would expect. Everyone must have gone back inside by now. They would be in the great hall, eating and drinking, trying to recover from the night's efforts.

She flexed her fingers and toes slowly, carefully, keeping her attention fixed on the man standing a few feet away from her. Why was he there and not bent over her? Had he heard something? Or was he watching for someone else to join him? That thought chilled her. If he was, she had very little time to save herself.

Screaming wouldn't help. By the time any of the exhausted people in the keep heard her and came out to investigate, she'd be dead. But she wasn't bound. And she'd tucked her eating knife into its pouch on her belt. If she moved quickly enough, she could surprise him.

Could she do it? Kill him before he killed her? She reached slowly for her small blade. She'd have to sneak up behind him and stab him in the neck. That was her only chance. Her blade wasn't long enough to reach anything vital anywhere else.

Her fingers closed around the hilt and she stilled, breathing softly, not wanting to attract his attention. He took a cautious step forward and peered around the corner of the stone wall into the open bailey. Then he stepped back and flattened himself against the adjacent wall.

She lay quietly. Someone was coming, and judging by her captor's reaction, he didn't welcome whomever approached. But who?

Tavish would be looking for her! When he returned to the kitchen and realized she wasn't there, or in her mother's chamber, he'd search for her. He might have taken the time to alert her father and others, like Bhaltair. She didn't know how long she'd been unconscious. But it had to be Tavish. *Please, let it be Tavish.*

Would he recognize this place, too, and realize that danger lurked here? She wanted to call out, but not until she was sure he was the one approaching. She didn't dare let her captor know she was awake.

She saw him before her captor did, flattened as he was against the wall, and changed her mind. "Tavish, he's here!"

With a roar, her captor sprang from his hiding place and launched himself at Tavish. His arm extended; dirk aimed at the middle of Tavish's chest. But her warning had been enough. Tavish was ready for him, dirk in hand. He knocked her captor's blade away and buried his in the man's shoulder. "That is for Donal," Tavish told him, then punched him in the face with his free hand.

Yvaine heard a sickening crack.

Blood poured from the man's nose as Tavish pushed him back against the keep's wall, one hand on his chest, one hand still holding the dirk buried in his shoulder.

"Who are ye, in truth? Ye canna be loyal to MacKyrie, not and do something like this." Tavish growled his question as Yvaine stood and approached slowly. "Stay back, lass." When the man didn't answer, Tavish twisted his dirk's hilt a wee. The man paled.

"I'll ask ye only once more. Yer name."

"Duff." He choked and spat blood onto Tavish's arm.

"What clan are ye from?"

Certainty filled Yvaine. "He's a MacDuff," she said, eyeing him. "He almost slipped and revealed his true clan."

His shocked glance bounced from her back to Tavish. He seemed to wilt before her eyes, then he straightened, despite Tavish's grip on the dirk in his shoulder, and glared at her.

"I'm nay a MacDuff."

"Then who?"

"MacKyrie. The laird kenned me." He grimaced. "Best ye kill me here, or her husband will, later."

"Are ye the one who attacked MacNabb?" Tavish's insistence had no effect. The man pressed his lips together and didn't answer. Instead, he pushed off of the wall and tried to go for Yvaine, but he only drove Tavish's blade deeper.

She heard it hit bone and winced at the crack of another break.

"Ye willna die, so *wheesht* ye," Tavish warned him. "I'll take ye to the healer, then ye can tell yer tale to *my* da, the Lathan laird."

"I ken who ye are. Dinna bother." He pushed against the blade in his shoulder and grimaced. "Take this out and finish me."

"Why?" Yvaine had to ask. "Why did ye do this?"

"To have ye, of course."

"Why her," Tavish demanded. "There are many lasses in this keep."

The man looked her over and sneered. "I never had the daughter of a laird. I've watched ye for as long as I've been assigned within the MacKyrie keep, but ye paid nay attention to me. I couldna get to ye there. Here, I was going to make sure ye kenned who had ye. But then I heard *him* coming."

So he *had* been waiting for her to wake up. "The daughter of a laird..." Yvaine's voice trailed off, and she turned her troubled gaze to Tavish.

"The other one, the Lathan lass, is always watched by that big guard."

"That's why ye did this?" Tavish swore and yanked the man off of the wall. He swung his captive around before he had a chance to react, and wrapped his free arm across his neck. "Ye are tetched in the head as well as daft." He kept the dirk in place with his other hand and ordered, "Walk."

Yvaine followed, silent and shaken, surprised the man complied. The ache in her hand made her realize she still gripped the hilt of her small blade. She pried open and rubbed her cramping fingers.

They'd only gone a dozen steps toward the keep's door

when Tavish's captive tried to jerk out of his grip. He succeeded only in forcing the blade in his shoulder to carve into his chest. Blood spurted from the wound, and he spit bloody foam before he went boneless. Only Tavish's arm now under his chin kept him upright.

"Run for help, Yvaine. Go!"

She didn't argue. She gathered up her skirts and ran for the keep's door. Someone came around the opposite side of the keep's entryway just before she reached it. Bhaltair!

"Yvaine! We've been search—"

"Come!" She cried and grabbed his arm. "Tavish has the assassin. He's hurt."

Bhaltair followed her at a run.

Tavish had lost his grip on the man and was on his knees beside him. "He's bleeding out," Tavish said.

Bhaltair scooped him up and ran for the keep's door. Yvaine knew he'd get the man to the healer. But would he manage it in time, or would her attacker be too far gone for Aileana to help him—and to get answers from him?

"He's said he's a MacKyrie guard," Tavish muttered, his gaze on the distance. "Yer mother kenned him."

She turned to him. He was covered in blood, his dirk still gripped in his left hand dripped red on the ground below it.

"But we dinna ken any more about him than that."

His gaze sharpened on her. "Except this—he isna Kilgore."

TAVISH WAS CERTAIN HE'D NEVER FORGET THIS FEELING. KILLING A man in battle was somehow easier to bear. He'd had no intention to kill this man, but his captive had taken the decision from him.

"Are ye hurt?" Yvaine studied every part of him, but he

knew there weren't any wounds to see, only the other man's blood on his clothes.

"Nay. He never touched me." Not physically, anyway.

"Come," Yvaine said softly and held out her hand to him.

He bent and stabbed his dirk in the ground to clean it, then wiped some of the blood from his hands onto his breeches before he took her hand.

She pulled him up. They walked back to the keep that way, hand-in-hand. By the time they reached the great hall, Bhaltair was coming back from the herbal, also covered in the other man's blood. It was still early enough that few people were in the great hall, and those that were stopped what they were doing when they spotted Tavish and Yvaine enter.

Bhaltair saw them and shook his head. "Dead."

"My fault," Tavish said and dropped his gaze. He should have done better. No doubt Donal would have wanted to question the man. His father would have, too.

"Nay!" Yvaine cried. "Ye canna believe that. He jerked against yer hold and forced the dirk's blade deep into his chest. He wanted to die. He tried to get away from ye and instead, only succeeded in killing himself."

"Yer mother said the same," Bhaltair informed him. "Something about the angle of the wound. Broken ribs. She kenned what happened without being told. A wise woman, yer mother."

"We need answers. How did he wind up in the MacKyrie guard?" Tavish lifted his head and pinned Bhaltair with a glare. "We thought he was one of hers, or I never would have left him to guard the laird and Yvaine. Lass, I am sorry. I shouldha realized there was something wrong about him."

"Why should ye, when I didna?" She touched his shoulder and shook his head. "'Twas not yer fault."

"Did he set the fire?" Bhaltair asked, frowning.

Aileana and Donal came out into the great hall then. Donal

rushed to his daughter. Aileana went to Tavish and touched his face. "Ye did a very brave thing, lad. Ye saved Yvaine."

"I killed that man."

"Ye didna," Yvaine insisted again, this time from her father's side. "He killed himself."

"It doesna matter," Tavish told her. "If I killed him or nay, I'd do it again to save ye."

"Ach, Tavish, I'm sorry." Yvaine left Donal's side and rushed into Tavish's arms.

"Lass, I'm getting blood all over yer dress." He didn't care, but she might.

"I dinna care. Just hold me, Tavish. I need ye to do that."

He glanced over her head at her father, who nodded, then-Tavish wrapped his arms around her. "Gladly."

YVAINE HELD ONTO TAVISH, NOT CARING WHETHER HER FATHER approved or not. Reaction had set in and she trembled.Her knees had turned to water. Without Tavish to cling to, she'd fall to the floor. Now covered in blood, she'd scare her mother to death whenever she came down with the guard sent to fetch her. Better Yvaine stay right where she was, pressed against Tavish's chest. That way, most of the blood on both of them was hidden between them.

She suspected Tavish needed the comfort of her touch as much as she needed his. She was happy to give it. She'd pushed him away for too long, and for no good reason. She belonged in his arms, and he in hers. Her talent didn't tell her that. Her heart did.

"Yvaine!" Her mother's voice pulled her out of the warm, cozy stupor she'd fallen into in Tavish's arms. "There ye are. And Donal. Aileana? Tavish? What is going on? The guard wouldna tell me."

Yvaine turned her head to meet her mother's gaze but didn't pull away from Tavish's arms. "Dinna fash. 'Tis not our blood. The man who threatened me is dead."

With that, she looked up at Tavish, nodded and stepped back. He let her go. She turned, giving her mother the full view of both her and Tavish's clothes. "It was on Tavish. He got it on me," Yvaine said and shrugged. "I dinna care."

"Nor do I," Ellie said, coming forward to cup her daughter's cheek, "as long as both of ye are unhurt."

Yvaine touched the back of her head. "Only a little headache left. I just noticed it."

"He hit ye?" Tavish's aggrieved tone nearly made her laugh.

"How else would he keep me quiet?"

"Damn. I wish I *had* killed him."

"I'd be dead but for ye, Tavish. Ye changed the outcome of yer vision. *Dinna fash.*"

Aileana stepped forward and touched Yvaine's forehead. "Ah, just a moment."

She closed her eyes, and when she opened them, Yvaine realized her headache was gone. "Thank ye, healer," she said, then glanced at her father. "And for yer care of my da."

"I've had a great deal of practice tending to yer da," she said. "Now, if someone can fetch my husband, ye can tell him everything." She glanced at Bhaltair long enough to ask, "Will someone remove that body from my herbal?" Then she reached out and touched both Yvaine's and Tavish's cheeks. "The two of ye can get bathed and dressed first. As ye are, ye are going to scare the bairns."

18

To Tavish's great relief, the gathering ended the next day and it was time for the feast. From the pleased smile on his father's face as he entered the great hall, Toran felt the same. As he crossed the hall to join the rest of his family at the head table, he clasped arms and spoke to the lairds he passed, and bowed to the few wives who'd traveled with their men. Aileana, already seated, stood as he approached and smiled down at him. "Well done, Laird Lathan," she told him. The gathered lairds, guards, and clan members erupted into cheers and applause.

The purpose of the gathering had been achieved. Relations between the lairds were strengthened, and the information they'd shared gave them the opportunity to develop contingency plans for every move the King might make against—or for—the Highland clans. The Auld Alliance and the continuing strife with their southern neighbors in the Lowlands and in England were problems of longstanding. Adding religious strife spread by zealous reformers created complexities they were not equipped to address. Tavish wondered when—or if— the MacKyrie Seer, her daughter or he would see anything useful about them. Perhaps those issues were too far removed to trigger their visions. He had no way to know.

Toran climbed the two steps to the raised platform and went to stand by his wife. "Thank ye all for coming. Despite the difficulties some of our visitors faced, and for the sacrifices ye all made in traveling here, at this gathering, we renewed our commitment to defending each other. We are stronger for these bonds, and when trouble comes, as it has in the past, and as it surely will in the future, we will stand together. Now, let the celebration begin."

He took his seat to more applause, swept the hall with a satisfied smile, then signaled for the food to be brought in.

"'Tis good he doesna like to give long speeches," Yvaine said at Tavish's side. "If I smelled the scents coming from the kitchen much longer, I'd have to leave ye here and go beg from Cook."

Tavish chuckled. "Ye were never in danger of that," he told her. "Da never has liked long speeches. Even in the gathering, I think the other lairds talked more than he did. He kept them on track and didna let the discussions wander off topic. Only rarely, when I was in attendance, did he insert himself."

"I dinna believe ye."

"I do exaggerate," Tavish told her with a grin, "but only a wee. Ah, here comes supper."

The grand feast to celebrate the end of the gathering featured the venison and the smaller game the men brought back from the hunt, roasted, baked into pies, stewed and grilled. Fish from the burn, other vegetables and braised greens from the keep's walled garden, and a variety of sweets rounded out the meal. As the serving lasses entered the hall, the scents strengthened, and Tavish's stomach rumbled in response.

As he ate, he paid attention to the people at the lower tables. He didn't see any signs of trouble. Kilgore had never reappeared. Some assumed he'd left the area. The sense of unease that usually heralded danger was there, but so faint,

Tavish was certain it resulted only from his concern over the number of strangers in the great hall. Still, with Yvaine by his side, he would not let down his guard until all the other visitors left.

Tavish thought back to the day they'd collected the names of each man in the lairds' entourages. Ellie MacKyrie had not been present—she'd left to attend to her wounded husband. Yet it turned out the dead man was one of MacKyrie's own! Tavish heartily regretted that he'd died before they could question him. They didn't know if he had attacked Donal. If he had, he must have counted on the confusion of strangers in the keep to blend in and stalk his prey—first Donal MacNabb and then an easier target—Yvaine.

Still, what they did know of the man's actions had shaken the laird's family. Tavish could understand their disbelief that one with such close access to them could have done what he did to Yvaine. The laird had directed that he be buried in an unmarked grave. Tavish understood that, too.

Was he in league with Kilgore? Or was Kilgore innocent of everything they'd suspected of him? They still didn't know. Precautions were still being taken around the MacKyrie laird and her husband. Bhaltair maintained that no one knew for certain if Yvaine's attacker had acted alone, or if Kilgore was still in the glen or hidden somewhere in the Aerie. Tavish agreed.

Donal had laughed off that notion, but Bhaltair's suggestion had given Yvaine a bad moment. She told Tavish she'd imagined being confined in her chamber and not seeing him again before they left to return to MacKyrie. Instead, he sat next to her. Close enough to protect her if need be, but with her family and some of Bhaltair's guards close enough that they could not have a private conversation.

Tavish spent the meal sneaking looks at her. The longing glances she sent his way told him she felt the same. His sister,

Eilidh, sat on Yvaine's other side. From what Tavish could hear over the rumble of conversations echoing off of the great hall's stone walls, she was making the effort to be pleasant company, something his normally quiet twin would not do. But from the looks Yvaine kept giving Tavish, the person she wanted to spend time with was Eilidh's twin. He tried to bear their situation with good grace, but it was a struggle.

Suddenly, Tavish's sense of unease spiked. He managed to catch Bhaltair's eye, frown and raise a hand to his head, to let the big guard know he was sensing something. But what?

Everything in the great hall seemed normal. People were eating. Servants moved between the long tables with trenchers of food, cups and pitchers of drinks, and musicians had arrived to provide music for dancing after the meal. Tavish watched as they took their place in one corner of the great hall, looking for anything out of the ordinary.

Bhaltair was surveying the chamber, as well. Tavish noticed him rise from his table and move across the hall, speaking to several of his men as he went. He did it so casually, Tavish was certain no one noticed any tension.

Closer movement caught Tavish's attention. A servant moved behind the head table, arms laden, face turned away as he replaced and relit torches in the sconces along the rear wall that had burned down during the dinner. Then he turned around and leapt.

Kilgore!

Tavish twisted around in time to see the flash of the blade Kilgore plunged into Donal's back.

Tavish surged to his feet, pulled his dirk, and leapt for Kilgore.

Kilgore pulled his blade from Donal's back. Blood dripped as he brandished it to defend himself from Tavish's attack. Toran joined the fight from the other side and knocked Kilgore from the upper table's platform. From the corner of his eye,

Tavish saw his mother move to Donal, then he was too busy defending himself to note anything else.

Kilgore feinted at Toran and charged Tavish.

Tavish parried his blade and kicked his knee as he closed.

The man stumbled but did not fall. He kept coming.

Tavish felt the burn of a slice down his upper arm. He ignored it and grappled with his attacker, fighting for control of his blade.

Toran stepped in from behind Kilgore as he swung at Tavish again, still trying for a killing blow.

Tavish defended himself, determined to take this man alive. The fight carried them into the wall.

Kilgore stood with his back to it, waving his dirk from side to side in an attempt to hold off both Toran and Tavish. They were handicapped by wanting to capture him. He had no such compunction. He fought to kill. As one attacked, he'd engage, then fall back to take on the other.

But he was tiring, slowing, and Tavish's next attack got through his defense. Tavish's blade pierced his lower side, stunning him. When Tavish pulled out his blade, the wound bled freely. He wouldn't last long.

Toran took advantage and struck his arm.

Kilgore's dirk clattered to the floor. Wide-eyed, he watched it hit and skid aside, then sank to his knees, clutching his side.

Tavish kicked Kilgore's dirk out of his reach.

"Who are ye?" Toran demanded. "Why are ye intent on killing MacNabb?"

The man didn't answer.

Bhaltair had been right. There were more MacKyrie enemies here than the one they'd sentaway over the back of a horse to a lonely grave.

Tavish glanced around. His mother bent over Donal. Both Ellie and Yvaine knelt on his other side, solemn, but with fear-filled eyes as Aileana fought to save his life. The rest of the hall.

It had gone silent and still. A ring of men, Lathans and those of other clans, had surrounded the upper table's platform to the walls, preventing any attempt Kilgore might have made to escape, and bearing witness to his treachery.

"I asked ye a question. Who are ye?" Toran repeated.

At the sound of his voice, Yvaine left her father's side, quit the platform and joined them. "Why did ye do this? Why did ye attack my da three times? 'Twas ye every time, aye?"

Her voice seemed to awaken something in him. He lifted his head and grinned. "I'm the grandson of the man yer da killed. I'm glad he has a daughter. When he dies from my blow, ye can suffer as I have for all these years."

"Why here? Why now?"

She moved closer, forcing Tavish to take her arm and restrain her out of the man's reach. She shook with the emotions within her, emotions Tavish could only guess at. He glanced at his mother, but saw only her back as she bent over Yvaine's father. The MacKyrie had risen and stood by, pale, hands clasped in front of her waist, as if they alone kept her from again dropping to her husband's side and interfering with his mother's efforts—and his sister's. Eilidh's hand hovered on their mother's shoulder. She lent strength to the Healer's efforts.

Donal was in trouble.

"I am the MacDuff now my da is gone. Or I would be if yer mother didna control my people. My land. My mines. I came to get it all back."

"By killing my da?"

"To start. He murdered my grandsire—"

"Who was bent on raping my mother and forcing her to marry him. Until Donal stopped him. I ken the tale. They fought. Yer grandsire lost."

"Yer da murdered him."

"Nay. He didna. 'Twasna a fair fight, though. Yer grandsire

forced my da to fight several of his men all at once. He killed them all. Ye have tried twice before this to kill him from a distance, and failed each time."

"Not this time."

Yvaine fisted her hands on her hips. "Aye, ye have failed again. The healer has saved him. And I hope ye suffer the same fate as yer grandsire. Ye are nay better than he was. In fact, ye are less than he was. At least he met his fate face-to-face against my da."

Tavish glanced again to where his mother and sister worked, hoping Yvaine was right.

Her words seemed to change something within Kilgore. His bravado faded, leaking from his face like the blood leaking between his fingers from the wound Tavish had inflicted in his side, and he slumped. "MacNabb lives?"

"He does."

"Then I have failed my grandsire and my clan." He turned to Toran. "What will ye do with me?"

"If ye survive yer wound, ye belong to the MacKyrie laird, whose husband ye have tried three times to kill. Likely her judgement will be death by hanging. It would be mine."

The man paled, then rallied and straightened. "He lives," he protested.

"And since he lives, if she agrees, I will send ye to the sheriff for judgement. And punishment."

"I'll escape, and I'll keep coming after MacNabb. Once he's gone, the MacKyrie laird will be weak. The King will return MacDuff to me."

"Ye and nay others?"

"Killing MacNabb is my duty as laird."

"Ye are nay a laird," Tavish spat. "Ye are a coward and a failure."

"Did ye send the man who attacked me?" Yvaine suddenly sounded tired and small.

"Nay," Kilgore spat. "But he served his purpose, to divert ye from me. Ye thought ye were safe when ye killed him."

She backed away, and Tavish let her go. Her stricken look made him want to reach out and take her in his arms, but this was neither the time nor the place for that.

———

TORAN CALLED A COUNCIL OF WAR THE NEXT MORNING INCLUDING all of his family in residence, plus Ellie, Yvaine MacKyrie, and Donal MacNabb, who had spent another night in Aileana's care, Bhaltair and others. They looked tired as they filed into the laird's solar, but the wounded had been healed and everyone had rested as well as they could after the events of the last evening. Toran had escaped injury during the fight, for which they were all glad. Eilidh had healed the cut on Tavish's arm while their mother finished with Donal.

Again.

She'd kept him in a healing sleep overnight. As long as he stayed calm, she deemed him well enough this morning to take part in the meeting.

Their prisoner spent the night under guard after his wounds were treated with poultices, and bound. Toran refused to let Aileana or Eilidh heal him. "He will heal and live, or die, as God wills," Toran decreed. "The secret of yer abilities willna leave the Aerie with him," he told his wife and daughter. "Nor will I have ye suffer for a man who tried three times to kill Donal."

"If the man truly is the heir to MacDuff, should his people be told what happened to him?" Tavish hated to ask the question in front of the MacKyries, but they had to be thinking about it, and it would help settle matters to discuss it.

Yvaine opened her mouth, then closed it after she glanced at her mother, making Tavish regret asking the question.

Ellie's expression sharpened. "They are my people now, by right. Until I deem otherwise, they belong to me, not to some stranger who purports to be the grandson of the man who gave them to me."

Tavish nodded, "They are," he agreed quickly, not wishing to anger her. "But because of what they were..." He needed to stop talking. Yvaine had tensed, and her father's frown was growing fierce.

Toran shook his head as he thought, then finally said, "'Tis better to leave his disappearance a mystery."

"If he dies," Ellie said in her grim Laird MacKyrie voice, "then I agree he should be forgotten. Yer men can bury him with the other one."

The other one, not my former guard, or the traitor. Laird MacKyrie had already banished Yvaine's attacker—in her mind —from the clan. Or she simply meant to protect her daughter from being reminded about what he'd done. Tavish couldn't blame her.

"I see no sense in stirring up trouble for MacKyrie by making an issue out of this Kilgore's death," she continued. "If he lives, and if he had supporters among the former MacDuffs, then depending on the sheriff's decision, word will spread, and we can be sure that trouble will follow." She leaned her elbows on the table and clasped her hands in front of her. "There havena been any other attempts like his. After so many years, I believe he acted alone, out of pride—or for vengeance, as he claimed. But there was never any doubt that his claim is invalid. The marriage contract MacDuff forced me to sign was clear, even if it didna turn out the way MacDuff expected, with me dead, and MacKyrie under his control. His men saw what happened during the fight when he died. Donal acted in my— and his own—defense when the old laird challenged him. Afterward, his people were treated with mercy, and sent on their way to tell the rest of their clan the old laird was dead."

"Stories grow—and change with time," Donal remarked, "The old MacDuff had many sons and many bastards. This man could be the get of any of them. We canna ken if he would have been the heir, as he says he is, or nay."

"And we canna find out without raising more questions than we'll answer," Toran said. "I say leave it be."

"His wounds have been treated as well as any healer without our talents could do," Aileana said. "He will be tended while he remains here, though to do nay more goes against my instinct to heal his wounds. The sooner ye send him away for judgement, the better."

By that afternoon, Toran's courier carried a letter describing the events of the last week, their prisoner's treachery, and requesting the sheriff accept custody of him, and render justice for MacKyrie. Tavish expected days would pass before the courier returned with an answer.

He was glad, because the MacKyries, particularly Yvaine, would not leave the Aerie until that matter was settled one way or the other. Still, questions remained. What if there were more McDuffs who agreed with Kilgore? Would the Sheriff's justice be equal to what Toran expected the MacKyrie to demand? Or would Kilgore remain alive and a threat?

The prisoner's presence was hard on his mother and sister. The training Tavish had received in traditional methods and medicines made him the best healer to care for the man. His developing healing talent was as yet weak enough that he did not suffer from their compulsion to heal. So, he was tasked with changing the man's bandages, checking the condition of his wounds and making certain he received food and drink.

On the second day, despite the care he'd been given, Tavish discovered Kilgore had developed a fever. Tavish told his laird, who accepted the news with a grim nod. Then his gaze bored into his son's and he repeated his order that none of any Lathan healer's special talent was to be used to care for the prisoner.

Tavish refrained from revealing his condition to his mother, who would insist the fever gave her cause to intervene. Toran would not allow it, and Tavish would not let Kilgore become the cause of strife between his parents. The sooner the man was gone from the Aerie—to receive the Sheriff's justice, or dead of his wounds—the better.

By that afternoon, most of the visiting lairds and their retinues were gone. Some faced longer trips home than others, but all had neglected their clans for a week or more to travel to the Aerie and attend the gathering. They left as they'd arrived, without fanfare, accompanied by their guards and retainers.

Tavish feared that Yvaine would be eager to return to MacKyrie. He didn't like the thought of her making the long trip back with only a retinue of guards to protect her. Without him. Nor did he like the idea of her living there with the threat of vengeful former MacDuffs hanging over her father's life, and perhaps the rest of her family's, too.

A great deal of trouble had come to the Aerie, if not with them, then because of them and their history. But thankfully, that trouble should be over, at least for now. No one knew if there was another MacDuff heir waiting for his chance to reclaim his clan's heritage. But after three failed attempts on Donal's life, Tavish felt certain they had caught the only man who'd followed them to the Aerie with that purpose in mind. What they might face at MacKyrie remained to be seen.

Time was short. If Tavish was going to speak to Yvaine, he must do so soon. Now that the commotion in the Aerie was dying down and he was no longer being pulled between his duty to his mother and to his father, he could spend more time with her. He needed to tell her how he felt, and to be sure she felt the same before he took any further steps. He wanted her with him. He needed her. And he could no longer contemplate a life without her in it. If she did not feel the same, he had very little time to convince her.

Yvaine gathered her meager belongings while Eilidh sat with her and told her stories about her father's history at the Aerie. She shared the tale of how her parents met at MacKyrie and the events that led to their wedding. She was able to fill in more of their history than Eilidh knew.

"Did he never go back to MacNabb? I dinna believe he ever did while he remained with Lathan," Eilidh told her.

Yvaine shook her head. "Not that I ken," she answered, wondering why he would leave his home as a young man and never return. She couldn't imagine leaving the MacKyrie glen forever. Even after she married, if she ever did, she expected to live there for much of the rest of her life.

But would she ever be given the choice? She and Tavish seemed to have gotten past their differences—those mostly her fault—and become close. He'd kissed her, and she felt at home in his arms. But would such small things lead to a life together? She couldn't say. And she was packing to return home without him, without an offer from him for her hand. With his twin sister for company instead of him. Where was Tavish? Suddenly, she wanted him near her.

But Eilidh cleared her throat, interrupted Yvaine's thoughts and pulled her back from the precipice of her useless musings.

"Not unless he went back after he moved to MacKyrie," Eilidh told her. "He always said he'd found his home here, and, because he was the youngest son, had left nothing behind at MacNabb. His skill as a warrior made him valuable and respected here, and he made an even better home at MacKyrie with yer mother."

Eilidh's comment about her father being the youngest son made her breath catch. She paused in folding a garment to follow the thought that consumed her. Tavish was also a youngest son. What did he have in his life that would give him a future like her father's—a future where he was needed and respected for his own strengths and skills, not just his family's?

Would he be a Seer like her mother, consumed with some other important work, or follow his inclinations where they led him, like her father had done, to a life and a family he loved?

At MacKyrie? With her?

"Are ye well, Yvaine?"

Eilidh's voice interrupted her thoughts yet again.

"Do ye need me to do anything for ye?"

Eilidh stood and reached toward her, but Yvaine backed away. "Nay, but thank ye. I am well. Simply overcome with sadness at the thought of leaving ye and yer family."

"And my twin, perhaps?"

Dare she admit it? The thought of leaving Tavish hurt most of all. But could she tell his twin, his closest sibling? Should she?

"Dinna fash," Eilidh said softly. "I can see it on yer face. Do ye love him?"

Yvaine collapsed onto the bed, seated and clutching the once-folded garment to her chest in a wrinkled mass. "I must. He cared for me even before he met me, in his visions, trying to protect me, to save my life. How can I not love a man like that? And I was horrid to him at first, accusing him of all sorts of ridiculous, insulting things. But he forgave me and continued to do as much as I would let him—and more—to keep me safe."

"Ye do love him."

"I do." The revelation saddened her even more. "Tell me, then, how can I leave him?"

"My brother is a responsible man, and a protective one. I can see where yer independent streak and his nurturing side might clash." Eilidh settled beside her on the bed, then reached out and began rubbing circles on her back, exactly the way Tavish would do it. The parallel brought tears to her eyes. "Perhaps 'tis best if ye do leave. Then my brother will realize how much he misses ye, how much he needs ye, and he will follow ye to MacKyrie and claim ye there."

"How can ye accept the idea of losing him to me and to MacKyrie so calmly? Ye are so close."

"Aye, we are. We always have been, from the womb. But we've always kenned that one day, we would go our separate ways, fall in love and marry others who would become just as important to us as each other. Our bond will always be there. Just as the triplets have gone their separate ways, yet they will always be special to each other. Besides, I wouldna lose him. I would gain a new sister in ye."

"I wish I was as close to my brother as ye are to yer family."

"Why do ye think ye are not?"

"Michiel is the heir. He has been raised to one day succeed our mother. My brother spends most of his time with her, and the rest with her oldest friend in the clan, his namesake, on the training ground. They learned long ago that my brother does not take direction easily from our father, even if he is one of the foremost warriors and arms masters. Since my da trained the elder Michiel, Da only steps in once in a while."

"What about ye?"

"My visions happen during sleep, and do not require the same investment of time with Mother as the Seer. She must devote more attention to Michiel as the heir to the laird. So, I am closer to Da."

"And has he trained ye to fight?"

"A lass?" Yvaine tried to put some incredulity into her voice, but Eilidh's laugh told her she failed. "Very well, aye, he has. And I am skilled in some weapons, but as I learned a few days ago, a man's size and weight can still overpower me."

Eilidh gave her a solemn nod. "I am so sorry that happened to ye." She reached out and took Yvaine's hand.

"And I am glad it didna happen to ye. Or any other lass

here. I escaped because Tavish was searching for me after he couldna find me in either of the two places he expected I'd be. Another lass might not have had someone looking out for her, and the result would have been much worse."

"Aye, it might have, but it wasna. In time, ye will remember only a brief moment of fear and then Tavish's care for ye will fill yer heart yet again."

Eilidh's voice had taken on a depth, a strength, that Yvaine had never heard before.

"I said some terrible things to him, even then," Yvaine confessed.

"They, too, will fade, and yer heart and mind will be left full with Tavish's love for ye."

Yvaine felt distracted but better, and realized Eilidh was right. Her fear of those memories, along with the memories themselves, were already fading. "Thank ye, Eilidh. I can feel ye are right."

Voices sounded in the hallway. Eilidh released her hand and stood. "I've interrupted yer preparations long enough, and I hear our mothers coming near."

Yvaine nodded and stood, unable to shake off the sudden lethargy that had filled her with Eilidh's assurances. "Best we go see—"

A knock at the door interrupted her. "Come," she called out as the door opened. "Ah, there ye both are," her mother said. "I'm sorry to interrupt ye, but Yvaine, yer da and I have something to discuss and ye need to be involved. And Eilidh…"

Aileana stepped forward, glanced at both young women and nodded. "I have a task for which I need Eilidh's assistance."

Yvaine turned to Eilidh. "Thank ye again," she told her. "I will think on yer advice."

Eilidh nodded and went to join her mother in the hallway.

Yvaine and Ellie crossed the hall to her parent's chambers.

Before the door closed behind them, she heard Aileana ask Eilidh a question.

"What did ye do, daughter?"

"Only a little," Eilidh answered, "and only what she needed."

Only what I needed? That made no sense to Yvaine. Eilidh hadn't done anything. She and Eilidh had simply talked.

19

Yvaine sat with her mother and father in their chamber as they discussed how to prepare for any threat that they must deal with when they got home—and on the way there. She fought to pay attention. The lethargy that filled her with Eilidh's reassuring words still ruled her, making her head muzzy and her breathing slow and measured, as if she neared sleep. Yvaine recalled enough to hope Eilidh was right. Her parting words as she and her mother walked down the hall still resonated in her mind. Yvaine had no idea what prompted Aileana's question, or what Tavish's sister had meant by her reply. Perhaps she'd get a chance to ask her later.

And later, if she had a chance to relate the conversation between her parents to Tavish, she'd tell him simply that her father was not willing to dismiss the possibility of more trouble waiting for them, and would ensure that they had sufficient escort home to deal with an army. Once there, her mother was reluctant to stir up trouble by making enquiries among the former MacDuff elements she controlled. If they discovered a reason at home to investigate, they would have to be extremely circumspect.

They had received no word from MacKyrie of dangers yet to be faced. Her brother did not share the Sight and would not be alerted by a vision. Likely nothing had occurred to concern either her brother or the older Micheil. Her mother surprised her by agreeing with her father that their troubles might not have ended. "We will have much to discover when we return to MacKyrie—carefully," she finally said, ending the discussion.

Yvaine took that as permission for her to leave. She headed down to the great hall and met Tavish as he came out of his father's solar. "Are ye well?" He looked tired, and still tortured by the death at his hands and another impending, even if neither had been his fault.

"Aye, now that I see ye," he answered. "Will ye walk with me?"

She smiled, glad that Tavish seemed eager to spend time with her, even though she'd been nothing but trouble for him. "Of course."

He offered his arm. "We have much to talk about."

She thought quickly back to the fight. Which of his arms had been injured? She didn't want to do more damage. Carefully, she wrapped her hand around his forearm. "We do?"

He led her out into the bailey but turned her toward the gate rather than farther into the bailey toward the kirk. She didn't want to revisit that area any time soon, and was glad Tavish didn't either. He surprised her when he escorted her out of the gate and started down the path to the glen.

"We willna go all the way down. I just thought ye might enjoy being outside the Aerie's walls, even if only this far, for a change."

"Ye were right," she told him, setting aside her memory of him carrying her up this very path. He'd done what her father demanded, and apologized for it. She had no doubt he'd been sincere when he stood up to her father and refused ever to harm her that way again. That had been the moment when her heart had opened to him. "Thank ye. This is a beautiful place, especially now that the glen is mostly empty again."

"And the damage done by tents, men and horses will be hidden soon by the first snow. By spring, 'twill be as if it never happened."

"I hope, for yer sake, that ye can put it behind ye much sooner than that," Yvaine told him, then turned back to study the peaks of the surrounding mountains and let the emotions filling her throat and tightening her chest subside. She meant more than the damage to the glen by her words. Tavish had not been the same since her attacker died so horribly. In truth, neither had she. Having to tend her father's attacker could not be helping Tavish to move past it.

Needing to distract herself, she responded to his comment about the encroaching winter. "MacKyrie may see heavy snow even sooner than ye. We should leave soon."

"Must ye?" He stopped and took both of her hands in his. "I dinna want ye to go. Yvaine. I care about ye. I have since I first saw ye in a vision. I felt I kenned ye even before I met ye. And after what we've been through these last days, my feelings for ye have grown."

Tingles spread along her nerves, bringing everything into sharper focus. What was he leading up to? "I have feelings for ye, too, Tavish. Ye did everything ye could for me, even when I was terrible to ye. And ye saved my life. Twice. I'm sorry for how I behaved."

"I couldna let anything happen to ye, not if I could stop it. When I thought I'd lost ye, I realized how important ye have become to me. I hope I am to ye, as well." He paused and swallowed. "I love ye, Yvaine. I dinna want ye to leave me. I want ye in my life." He cupped her cheek with one hand. "I dinna ken how many ways to say it, so I'll just say it simply. I want ye to be my wife."

She sucked in a breath. Joy burst through her, making her

heart beat as fast as a bird's and heat rise in her chest. Her fingertips tingled as she lifted them to cover her lips.

"Ye dinna have to answer now," Tavish said. "And if ye feel ye must return home to MacKyrie to think on my offer, I willna claim to like it, but I will understand. These feelings we have between us have grown quickly, despite all we've been through, or perhaps because of it all. I ken that. Sometimes a link can be forged in the heat of battle that doesna survive its end." When her eyes widened, he hastened to add, "But I dinna think that will be the case for us. I need ye, Yvaine. We need each other. And I do love ye, more than I kenned I could love anyone, before I met ye."

She lifted her hand from her mouth and turned it to stop him, the urge to laugh with glee nearly stealing her ability to speak. "Tavish, nay. I dinna need to wait. I feel the same for ye." She clasped her hands in front of her chest. "I will marry ye with a glad heart. I've never wanted another man before ye. I never will again." She reached up and caressed his face, unable to go another moment without touching him. "We are seers. We are meant to be together. To learn and grow together. We have already seen that we are stronger together. Whether we live here or at MacKyrie doesna matter. I only care that I am with ye. Ye are the man I want by my side."

He pulled her to him and enfolded her in his arms. "I need ye by mine, Yvaine. To love and cherish for all of my life. To be the mother of my bairns. To make a home with me. A life with me. Only ye."

His gentle kiss whispered over her temple as he spoke, then her eyelid, before he took her mouth. She could feel the longing in him to hold her like this forever. His desires mirrored her own. She wanted the life he described, the two of them together, always.

When he broke the kiss, she told him, "Then we shall. Yer

words have filled me with joy, Tavish. What we have between us may have grown quickly, but it is true and right. I feel that, too."

He released her and they started back up the path. Yvaine fought down a giggle at the thought of their parents' surprise when they learned of this. "If we are to go on as we have started, I wonder, how quickly can we wed?"

"If we could enlist our priest's help to keep our families from wanting a big ceremony and celebration, we could wed as soon as tonight." He shook his head. "Not that he'd succeed. Or we could handfast, then wed any time after that. What do ye wish for?"

"I think ye were right. We have much to talk about."

TAVISH TOOK YVAINE TO SPEAK TO THEIR MOTHERS. ELLIE HAD taken to spending time with Aileana and Eilidh in the herbal. All three were there when they arrived.

"We have news," Yvaine announced, hand-in-hand with Tavish. She fought to keep a smile from her face, but her joy was too great and it broke through.

"I kenned it," Ellie said, a bright smile lighting her eyes.

Yvaine turned to Tavish. "This is what comes of having a Seer for a mother. 'Tis hard to keep a secret or a surprise."

"The same is true when ye have a meddlesome healer for a mother, too," he said, catching his mother's gaze and grinning. Then he turned back to the MacKyrie Seer. "We are happy to confirm to ye that ye saw true. We wish to be wed. Yvaine has agreed to be my bride."

"Ach! How wonderful!" Eilidh rushed forward and embraced them both, then looked around. "Do ye mean both our mothers already kenned it? Why does no one ever tell me anything?"

"'Twas not our place to do so," Ellie answered with a satisfied smile. "'Twas yer brother's and Yvaine's."

"Well, I'm happy about it, either way," Eilidh announced. "Have ye told da and Donal?"

"Told us what?"

Toran's voice startled Yvaine and she glanced around to see him and her father at the herbal's door.

"This is where ye all are hiding," Toran continued. "What have ye not told us?"

Donal elbowed Toran. "Look at their faces. Canna ye guess?"

"Yvaine and I wish to marry," Tavish announced. "Sooner rather than later."

Both men looked to their wives and Toran asked, "Did ye put them up to this?"

Aileana shook her head. "Nay, but Ellie saw that it would happen."

"Ye did? And ye didna tell me? How long ago?"

Donal's aggrieved question made Ellie grin.

From the intent look on her face, Yvaine wanted the answer to that, as well.

"Before we even left MacKyrie, Husband. Before I began to use the valerian and stopped being able to see. I kenned this trip could end well for all of us, though there were times I lost faith in that knowledge." She reached out to her husband and grasped his hand.

"And ye didna tell me?" Yvaine lifted a hand to her throat. "Ye kenned how worried I was about da!"

"And ye ken our visions are not always reliable," Ellie said and shrugged. "I am sorry, but I thought it best to keep this to myself. I didna ken who ye might find who would make ye happy, only that ye might find him here. I had to let the two of ye come to each other in yer own way, at yer own pace. Though 'twas hard to keep silent about such good news."

They spent the rest of the evening discussing the wedding. Tavish sided with Yvaine's attempts to keep the event small so it could take place soon, but their wishes were only partly agreed to. She wasn't certain if she was glad or disappointed that both sets of parents rejected the idea of handfasting in favor of a wedding, but she did enjoy, as the next few days passed, watching the whole keep join in the planning and preparations.

Despite the furor of the wedding preparations, Tavish insisted on having some private time with Yvaine while they waited for fast riders to take the news to Tavish's older brother and sister. They spent much of it in the keep's walled garden among the last of the summer flowers and fruits. "Of yer brothers and sisters, this leaves only Eilidh unwed," Yvaine said during one of their private times. "Does she have a special someone?"

"If she does, she has been most quiet about it. I canna say."

"If she doesna, we will have to help her find her love."

"Nay, lass. Eilidh would resent the interference, no matter how well-meant it was. Best to let her find her own way. As we have. Yer mother was wise to keep this from us. We had enough time to learn to love each other. Eilidh deserves no less."

"Ye are right, of course." She let go of his hand and wrapped her arms around her middle. "I canna believe how our lives have changed in such a short period of time. What else can come to us, I wonder?"

"Whatever comes, we will weather it or revel in it together, ye and I," he promised, enfolded her in his arms and kissed her.

"We barely ken each other," Yvaine said once they broke off the kiss. "I met ye only a fortnight ago."

"And yet I met ye weeks before that, in my visions." He lifted her chin with a gentle finger. "We ken each other well enough to wish to spend the rest of our lives together. Does that not give ye confidence that we will go forward well together?

"Ye give that confidence to me, Tavish. No matter the circumstances, 'tis ye I look to for our future."

"And I look to ye. Is that not how a good marriage is supposed to work? I have only my parents to rely on, but they are stronger together than apart. As are yers."

"That is true. We've both have good examples to follow."

"And someday, we will be the ones setting a good example for our bairns to follow."

Yvaine shivered. "I can barely credit that someday we will be parents and be responsible for raising bairns of our own. I dinna ken if I am ready."

Tavish laughed. "Is anyone ever ready? Look to Drummond, who married a lass with a six-year-old bairn. Suddenly he is father to a son. And I've never seen him happier."

Yvaine nodded. "I suppose not. Not unless they've had to wait a long time for a bairn."

"We have begun together quickly. Perhaps the rest will follow much the same way. Would ye mind?"

Yvaine's smile warmed him. "Nay, I wouldna mind. I hope it will."

———

Yvaine's insistence that she didn't want a fuss fell on deaf ears. The wedding preparations were still underway at the end of another sennight.

First, there was the matter of a suitable dress. Then for an appropriate wedding feast, the men had to go hunting again to restock the larder depleted by the recent gathering of lairds and all their men. The news and invitations had been sent toJamie and Lianna, Tavish's two-years-older triplet siblings with Drummond, both of whom had married away from the Aerie.

Still, she had to say something. After the evening meal, she knocked on the door of her parents' chamber. "The Lathans have been so kind," she told them once they were all seated before the hearth, "that I dinna wish to be difficult, but what they and ye, Mother, have in mind for this joining is going to take forever." She turned to her father. "Canna ye talk some sense into them? We want to do this soon. We could even handfast."

"Daughter, this romance between ye and Tavish developed very quickly and under difficult circumstances."

Her heart sank. She'd counted on him to be her champion. "Da, I ken ye mean well, but ye are not helping." She had learned at an early age that her father could not stand up to a lass's tears. She would resort to that if she must.

"Perhaps taking this time to reflect is wise."

"Ye must make many decisions, such as to think on where will ye live while ye continue to mature yer talent as seers," her mother told her. "'Tis best done at MacKyrie."

Yvaine shook her head. "But Aileana insists that Tavish continue to develop his healing talent, as well. That, he must do here, at least for now."

"Why not return to MacKyrie while ye think on this?" Her mother gave her an understanding smile. "Ye can celebrate a betrothal for now. If 'tis meant to last, Tavish can come in the spring to work with me—and ye—to develop yer abilities as seers. Ye can marry then."

Her father caught his wife's gaze. "I dinna wish to disagree, but I think that 'tis wiser for now, for Yvaine to remain here. She will be safer at the Aerie, in case there is another MacDuff with a grudge against me—or against ye as MacKyrie laird."

"Kilgore is in the sheriff's custody," she objected. "He claimed to be acting alone."

"Dare we believe him?"

"Then I will remain here," Yvaine insisted. "Ye can stay for the wedding and return home after ye think 'tis safe for ye to travel, but before the snows close the pass into our glen."

"'Tis true, I must return soon," her mother fretted. "Michiel has had the burden of acting for me for too long."

"If yer mother were not the laird," her father said, "I might be open to a longer stay at the Aerie. Not for a wedding, mind ye, but to draw out any others with ideas like our former prisoner's." He reached over and squeezed his wife's hand. "But I must bow to the laird's wishes to return home. If trouble is coming to MacKyrie, we must be there to deal with it."

Yvaine's parents shared a look, then nodded. "So, we will wait for Tavish's brother and sister to arrive," her mother said, "but yer da and I will return to MacKyrie soon after ye are wed."

"Wonderful," Yvaine agreed with a grin. "Do ye think another sennight will see this done? Without so much fuss?"

"I dinna ken. I will speak to the Lathans, and ye can finish any preparations that are important to ye while we wait."

20

Yvaine had managed to convince her parents to go forward with her wedding. But winning them over was only the first step. She suspected her da's argument that in very few weeks, the passes into the MacKyrie glen would be impassible carried more weight than her and Tavish's eagerness to be wed.

Tavish's parents wanted to invite friends and family from all over the Highlands, including calling back some of the recently departed lairds. Tavish estimated doing so would delay the wedding for at least a month—the time it took for the invitations to go out and guests to arrive. Thankfully, Eilidh was on Yvaine's side. She and her twin brother soon managed to rein in their parents, but Yvaine remained convinced the parents were delaying to give them time to be certain of what they were doing.

As a result, the wedding took place in the great hall ten days later. Yvaine drew the line at using the kirk, since it sat next to where her attacker had meant to ravage and kill her and where he had killed himself on Tavish's blade. Those events were too recent, too fresh in both their minds. When the priest agreed to change the venue, Yvaine breathed a sigh of relief.

The Lathan's seamstress had worked miracles and made a beautiful dress for Yvaine to wear for her special day. The ivory silk underdress was complemented by an overdress of so deep a blue it was nearly black, with an open skirt and slashed sleeves that let the luster of the underdress shine through with each move she made.

There were more than enough Lathans in residence to make for a celebration, including Toran's cousin Jamie, who remained behind after most of the other lairds left the gathering, and his namesake Jamie, the youngest triplet, without his wife.

The triplet sister, Lianna, came with her husband, David MacDhai. As wedding presents for Drummond and Morven, and for Tavish and Yvaine, they brought some of the most beautiful young horses Yvaine had ever seen. She'd heard the tale of David's desperate return to the Aerie last year seeking help to save the horses that were his clan's lifeblood. Their gifts must be some of the horses that Lianna had saved. The Lathan laird's eyes lit up when he saw them, as did her father's.

Just before the evening meal was to be served, everyone but Yvaine and Eilidh gathered in the great hall near the hearth. Yvaine peeked from the top of the stairs at Tavish and his brothers, who stood at the front of the group. They looked so much like each other that they must confuse people all the time. But not her. She would know Tavish anywhere.

Her father left the Lathans and waited at the bottom of the stairs to escort her to her betrothed. Eilidh, who had helped Yvaine get ready, went first. As she reached the bottom of the stairs Donal took her hand and kissed her cheek, then sent her forward to stand with her older sister and her parents.

Yvaine followed then, her heart in her throat. Her blood sang in her veins, whether from nerves or eagerness, she wasn't sure. Perhaps both. As he had done for Eilidh, her father took her hand and kissed her cheek, then offered his elbow. She was glad of his support. Her knees suddenly felt weak and her whole body trembled. The heat in her face told her she'd blushed a bright red. Everyone could see her, and putting her emotions on display that way would normally upset her, but today, somehow, she didn't mind.

Donal escorted her through the group of Lathan well-wishers and guards, who'd parted to make an aisle for them through the middle, and put her hand in Tavish's. She didn't miss the warning glint in the look he gave Tavish. Nor the smile that Tavish gave him back. She understood the message as well as they did.

Take good care of her or else.

Of course, I will. I love her.

She smiled at her imaginingsas she turned to Tavish. He took her other hand, too.

"My beautiful Yvaine," he murmured, his gaze fixed on her eyes. "How I've looked forward to this day."

"In dreams, or in the real world?"

"In both. I'm glad it has finally arrived. We will have years to spend together in the real world. And perhaps, even more as well if we learn to dream together."

The priest cleared his throat. "Are ye ready?"

"Aye!" They answered in unison, then Yvaine gave in to the laughter bubbling up her throat. Tavish grinned at her, then turned back to the priest. "Go on, if ye will."

The ceremony was mercifully short. Yvaine had requested that, too. Before she knew it, the priest pronounced them man and wife and told Tavish to kiss her.

"With pleasure!" He met her gaze, silently asking her permission, then dipped his head and claimed her lips after she smiled.

Yvaine kissed him back, losing herself in the familiarity of his taste and the warmth of his firm lips on hers. Then she broke the kiss and tilted her head aside to whisper in his ear, "I think we're being watched."

Tavish chuckled and nodded. "Aye. Best we save the rest for later." He straightened and turned them to face their families. "I'm honored to present to ye my wife, Yvaine MacKyrie Lathan!"

The hall filled with applause and shouts of congratulations. After being hugged by more people than she could count, or so it seemed, and after a toast with MacKyrie whisky to the new couple that must have put a serious dent in the cask her parents had brought for the Lathan laird, Yvaine was glad to see the servants appear with the feast.

Tavish led her to the head table. Tonight, they would take the center seats, with her parents on her side and Tavish's on his. Everyone else filled the trestle tables below them.

He gave her the choicest bites from their trencher, but did not make the mistake of trying to feed them to her. She was Donal MacNabb's daughter, and Tavish knew it very well. She could take care of herself. But she let him indulge her when the sweets appeared.

Afterward, everyone pushed back tables, clearing the floor for dancing. She loved all the dances, but even more doing them with Tavish. And he looked like he was having a wonderful time, too.

But after another toast to the happy couple, he suggested they take their leave. "I dinna want ye to be too tired to enjoy the rest of the night," he whispered to her.

Bees suddenly erupted from slumber in her belly and buzzed along her bloodstream. She took a breath, determined not to let nerves ruin the happy evening they'd enjoyed so far. "Then let us depart."

They couldn't just sneak away. They had to climb the stairs in full view of the entire great hall. They were treated to clapping and cheering, but, in accordance with Lathan custom, no one tried to follow them. Of that, Yvaine heartily approved.

THEY'D MOVED TO ONE OF THE LARGE SUITES IN A DIFFERENT tower, away from Yvaine's small chamber across from her parents, and from Tavish's equally spare chamber. Tavish led his new bride along the hallways connecting the towers, pointing out his parents' and Eilidh's chamber when they passed them.

Tavish was glad to see his belongings were already in their new home. Yvaine had little to move, but once her parents returned to MacKyrie, they would send her things to the Aerie.

"Do ye like it?"

Yvaine surveyed the outer sitting room with its hearth, comfortable chairs and a small table under the window, then stepped through the doorway into the sleeping chamber. It held a bed easily large enough for both of them and two chests. A small hearth provided light and warmth when the shutters were closed. Tavish was confident he and Yvaine would quickly make it theirs.

A bottle of MacKyrie whisky, another of fine French wine, and a pitcher of cider waited on the table in the sitting room, along with cups, oat bread, honey and cheese. "We can live on that for a few days," Tavish remarked.

Yvaine smiled. "Will we cause talk if we do?"

"We'll cause talk, no matter what we do," he told her with a grin.

"Well, then," she said and lifted her chin, "let's make it worth our while, husband."

Tavish caressed her soft cheek and nodded. "I ask this only to treat ye as ye wish to be treated, wife. Are ye untouched?"

Her cheeks bloomed a lovely shade of pink. "I am. Until ye,

I was also unkissed. I find that activity pleasing and think we should do much more of it."

Tavish didn't have to be told twice. He pulled Yvaine to him and took her mouth, determined to please her in every way a husband could. Once they stopped letting their fears keep them apart, their romance had blossomed quickly. Tavish had no doubts they were meant to be together. She'd come to him many times in his visions. He'd saved her life—twice, and her mother finally admitted she had seen them together, happily wed, long before they met—though she hadn't known he was the man with her daughter. He wished he could have seen that vision, but Ellie had told them that only rarely did she see anything that affected her directly. Tavish knew the future they built together would not be influenced by their sight, but by their love for each other and the family they might create.

YVAINE RELISHED THE TOUCH AND TASTE AND SCENT OF HER husband. His mouth moving over hers was firm, moist and warm. He teased her ear, her throat, and the sensitive juncture of her shoulder. She clung to him, afraid her legs would not support her.

She couldn't fathom how he had become so necessary to her, and so loved. When she first met him, she thought him arrogant and annoying. How quickly events had forced her to see Tavish for who he really was. Caring, determined, honorable. Protective and loving. She should have known by the way his clan respected him and interacted with him that she could trust him. But she'd been blinded by her own fears, her own imaginings and visions. What a fool she'd been.

Here in her arms was the man she'd waited for. The man she'd dreamed about while watching the full moon rise over the Aerie's towers. The man she would love until the day she died.

As Tavish pulled her tightly against him and caressed her from shoulders to the curve of her hips, strange sensations raced along her limbs. Aye, here was the man who would show her what it meant to be not just a lass, but a woman. She cradled his face in both her hands and locked her gaze with his. "Ye ken I love ye, Husband. Do ye have any idea how much?"

Tavish smiled and her heart sang to see the joy in his expression.

"As much as I love ye?"

"And more. More than I ever kenned I could love anyone."

"I'm glad of that, Wife. I feel the same. I will love ye all our lives. I vowed it and I ken it to be true."

"We will have a wonderful life together."

"Have ye seen it?"

"I dinna need to. I feel it. And now, I want to feel ye, with me, inside me. Make me yers forever, Tavish. I need to be yers, and ye mine."

"Gladly, Yvaine."

He slipped her wedding finery from her body, then shed his own. Yvaine marveled at his sculpted form, evidence of a life spent in hard work and training as a warrior, though his path lay elsewhere. Another truth she recognized now was that Tavish would prepare for any eventuality that might come to them, good or bad. He could keep her safe.

"Ye are even more beautiful than I could have imagined," he told her, hoarse with the emotions filling him as he gazed at her unclothed form.

"And ye are even more intimidating," she said and gave a nervous laugh.

"*Dinna fash*. I have promised to take great care with ye, and I will. I want ye to enjoy this night, my love. And many more to come." When she nodded, he lifted her effortlessly and settled her on the bed.

To keep from trying to cover herself, she reached for him. Apparently, it was the right thing to do. He smiled and stretched out beside her, then took her into his arms and held her closely along the entire length of his body. Heat filled her, his added to her own. The warmth he gave her softened her muscles and let her relax in his embrace. She wrapped an arm around his waist and stroked his back, tracing each rib, each ridge of powerful muscle, then let her fingers slip down his side to his hip. His groan told her he liked her touch. "I dinna ken what to do, Tavish," she finally admitted. "Teach me."

"Gladly," he told her and rolled her onto her back. "Let me show ye." At her nod, he kissed her, then trailed warm breath to nip at her earlobe, and trace his tongue down her neck to her shoulder. He nipped her there. The brief pain startled her and heightened her senses as he nibbled his way down her chest and took one tight nipple in his mouth.

He sucked gently and Yvaine arched into his mouth, wanting more. While he suckled at her other breast, his fingers traced lazy circles down her belly to her thighs.

Instinctively, she parted them for him. Strange new sensations filled her. She wanted something, but she didn't know what. She moaned as his mouth followed the path his fingers had drawn, down her belly to her thighs, where he kissed the inside of each knee, then moved upward while he stroked down her legs. She didn't know which sensation pleased her more. No one had ever touched her in this way.

Then he kissed her center, and Yvaine lost the ability to think. She could only feel. She skimmed along the surface of these new sensations until Tavish took her deeper, exploring her with teeth and tongue, and with fingers that he slipped inside her.

"Ye are already wet, my love, but ye are not yet ready for me," he murmured. "Soon, though. Soon."

She didn't know what would happen soon, but then he stroked her deeply while his tongue delved firmly along her private place. Suddenly, she knew. Her body spasmed with pleasure so intense, she cried out and arched against him. He continued to stroke her until the spasms passed and she collapsed, boneless, in his arms.

Then he took her. Slowly, gently, as he'd promised, he entered her until he paused. "This may hurt, my love, but only this once."

She nodded, secure in his desire for her.

He pushed through. Pain shattered her contentment, but only for a moment before it subsided. Tavish was fully in her, and she was now his. That knowledge made the small discomfort the most important pain she'd ever felt, and the most worthwhile. "'Tis gone, love," she told him. She was ready to experience everything Tavish could show her.

Tavish began to move. The delicious pressure built in her again, made even more delightful as he kissed her and whispered of his love for her. She crested again, and after a few more strokes, Tavish's breath caught and he paused, straining, as his own pleasure erupted in him. Then they collapsed, side by side, in each other's arms.

"Ye are mine now, Yvaine, love, my wife forever," he told her as he lifted a lock of hair that had fallen across her forehead and pushed it back out of her face. "I love ye, and will always take care of ye as best I can."

"I trust that ye will. And ye are mine, Tavish," she answered, "my husband forever. I love ye, and will always take care of ye, as best I can. I am where I always wished to be, even though I didna ken it when ye saw me smile at ye in yer visions. With ye."

"With ye," he affirmed. "Wherever we may go, and whatever we may do. Ye, and the bairns we may have will be the center of my life, my reason for everything I do. I will care for ye and protect ye. And love ye. Forever, my love."

EPILOGUE

A YEAR LATER

The last year had gone by so swiftly, Yvaine could scarce credit how like a fast-flowing burn the time had carried them along. They had remained at the Aerie for Tavish to continue his healer training with Aileana and his twin sister. Yvaine had made friends with the weavers, especially Morven, and had learned some of her techniques for creating beautiful, soft, even delicate fabrics.

The loom fascinated her. MacKyrie had a weaver, but she preferred her work to speaking with young lasses, even young lasses who were the laird's daughter. Yvaine had never had the chance to learn much about her craft. And the fabrics she made, while sturdy, could not compare to Morven's.

But mostly, she had spent time with the keep's animals, helping to train the many litters of puppies, large and small, whether they would help guard or hunt, or even comfort the people of the clan. The horses took to her as well. She was always called upon to assist with a foaling, or to help calm a horse being ridden for the first time. She had no talent for healing, but this affinity was, in its own way, useful, too.

Yvaine hated to leave the Aerie. But the time had come to

return to MacKyrie so that she and Tavish could continue to work with her mother and learn how to better control and interpret their visions. And she looked forward to continuing to explore her newly honed affinity for animals at MacKyrie.

Ellie had stayed in close touch through frequent letters to Yvaine and to Aileana. She was well, and completely free of pain. Aileana's explanation had sounded perfectly horrible to Yvaine, but it explained why her mother had had so much pain for so long. She was glad Aileana had been willing to help. And glad that Tavish's healing talent had strengthened over the past year. If her mother had any more pain, Tavish could monitor and help her, and send for Aileana or Tavish's twin, if need be.

"Are ye ready to go, love?" Tavish's voice startled her from her thoughts.

"Aye, just packing the last few things," she answered, glancing around to smile at him as he entered their sitting room from the hallway. "Are ye eager to be gone?"

"I'm eager to see the MacKyrie glen," he told her. "And to get there before the first snow."

"Ach, aye. The pass. Of course, ye are. We'll get there. I dinna recall ever seeing a snowfall this early in the season. *Dinna fash.* Da and his men will meet us halfway. Between our Lathan escort and them, there will be plenty of men to help clear a path for the wagons, if need be."

"Let's hope they willna need to."

Eilidh and Aileana came to the door. "Do ye need any help?" Aileana stepped into the sitting room and looked around. "Ah, ye've nearly finished packing."

"I think so," Yvaine answered. "Save ye and all the rest of the Lathans. I wish we could take all of ye with us. I'll miss ye."

"We'll miss ye, too, lass."

"And Tavish, too, of course," Eilidh added with a smirk at her brother.

"And ye will send word the moment ye ken ye are with child, aye?"

"We will, Mother," Tavish told her. "I wouldna have anyone attend Yvaine, save ye."

"What about me?" Eilidh sounded aggrieved.

"Or ye, aye, but Mother has more experience."

"And how am I to gain that if ye dinna call on me?"

"Dinna fash," Yvaine told her. "Ye will be welcome, too. Whenever ye can come, for whatever reason, we'll be pleased to see ye."

That seemed to mollify Tavish's twin. Yvaine took her hand, in case it hadn't. "I mean that, truly, Eilidh. We are sisters now, and I will always be glad to welcome ye."

The approving look Tavish gave her told her she'd said and done the right thing for his twin.

"We'll let ye finish," Aileana said. "The wagons are in the bailey. Yer da and brother have made sure they are loaded and ready for yer last few things. We'll see ye down there."

"We'll be there in a few minutes," Tavish told her, and she and Eilidh closed the door behind them as they left. "We canna delay any longer," he said once they were alone.

"I ken it. But I'm suddenly even more reluctant to leave. Yer family has been so good to me. I meant what I told them. I will miss them."

"I ken ye will," Tavish said and folded her in his strong arms.

She tucked her arms around his waist and clung to him. She never got tired of being held. He made her feel safer and warmer than she'd ever been anywhere else. "But our training is important if we're ever to be the seers we should become for our clans, and for that, we must work with my mother."

"'Twill be strange for me to be away from my family, but 'twill be an adventure, my love. One we take together."

Yvaine lifted her arms and cradled the nape of his neck. "I

will go to the ends of the earth if that is what ye wish, Husband. As long as I am with ye, I am home, safe and loved. All thanks to yer dreams."

"Nay lass. 'Tis because I love ye, and ye love me. Our love is real, not a dream. As long as we have each other, it willna matter where we are."

AUTHOR'S NOTE

Look for Book 5 in my Highland Talents Heritage series, HIGHLAND ECHO, Eilidh Lathan's story, in April 2023.

HIGHLAND ECHO (Highland Talents Heritage Book 5)

Eilidh Lathan is bound to the Aerie by the echo in her blood of her mother's healing talent and her love for one man. If only she had the courage to tell him—and he felt the same.

Bhaltair Lathan's intimidating stature makes him the ideal Lathan chief guard. But no matter how gently he treats Eilidh, he believes that she will never welcome him as her lover. Rather, she will forever view him as a warrior to be feared.

On a mission of mercy to a neighboring clan, deadly danger lurks. Bhaltair must save Eilidh from an unthinkable fate. Though their lives depend on trusting each other's strengths, he fears losing any chance of gaining her heart if he surrenders to his vengeful fury. Can the timid healer and the clan's most fearsome warrior find a love that will bind them forever?

ALSO BY WILLA BLAIR

Highland Talents Legacy

Highland Prodigy

Highland Memories

Highland Reckoning

Highland Dreamer

Highland Echo

His Highland Heart

His Highland Rose

His Highland Heart

His Highland Love

His Highland Bride

Highland Talents

Heart of Stone

Highland Healer

Highland Seer

Highland Troth

The Healer's Gift

When Highland Lightning Strikes

Sweetie Pie (A Candy Hearts Novella)

Waiting for the Laird

When You Find Love

ABOUT THE AUTHOR

Willa Blair is an award-wining Amazon and Barnes & Noble #1 bestselling author of Scottish historical, light paranormal and contemporary romance filled with men in kilts, psi talents, and plenty of spice. Her books have won numerous accolades, including the Marlene, the Merritt, National Readers' Choice Award Finalist, Reader's Crown finalist, InD'Tale Magazine's RONE Award Honorable Mention, and NightOwl Reviews Top Picks. She loves scouting new settings for books, and thinks being an author is the best job she's ever had.

Willa loves hearing from readers!
Contact her:
www.willablair.com
authorwillablair@gmail.com

Sign up for my Newsletter
Find links to the rest of my books

www.ingramcontent.com/pod-product-compliance
Lightning Source LLC
Chambersburg PA
CBHW050318110726
47899CB00007B/2285